a novel

POISON TWO

A FATAL ATTRACTION

K.D. HARRIS

PUBLISHER'S NOTE:
This book is a work of fiction.
Names, characters, businesses, organizations, places,
events and incidents are the product of the author's imagination or are used fictionally.
Any resemblance of actual persons, living or dead, events, or locales is entirely coincidental.

ISBN: 0-9823913-0-7
ISBN 13: 978-0-9823913-0-3
Cover Design: Davida Baldwin www.oddballdsgn.com
Editor: Advanced Editorial Services
Graphics: Davida Baldwin
Typesetting: Davida Baldwin
www.thecartelpublications.com
First Edition
Printed in the United States of America

What Up Babies,

It's Here! It's Here! Poison 2 has finally hit the shelves! I see K.D's growth as an author but moreover; I see her tenacity and spirit! She had my mouth opened the moment Nyse's wretchedness was reintroduced into this book. And in the end, delivered a sequel that I'm sure her fans will adore.

With that said, the Cartel Publications is proud to bring to you, Poison 2! Get comfortable, relax and delve into a story that's bound to entertain, page after page!

Lastly, as you know in every novel we publish, we pay homage to an author who has paved the way, or one we adore simply for his or her literary journey. So it is with great pleasure that we pay homage to a man that was voted as one of the "Most Underrated Authors". He's none other than,

"Moses Miller"

Moses *is* one of the greatest! Hands down! He's not only a brilliant novelist, but he's also a wonderful person and a force within the African American community. He doesn't just talk about change he is change. Moses has written great classics like, **The Trifling Times of Nathan Jones, The Game of Trife** and **Barack and Me**. Moses thanks for setting standards and being a shining example as an author, friend and man. We are in appreciation for all that you do.

Don't forget to visit us at our bookstore, Cartel Café & Books located at, 5011 Indian Head Highway, Oxon Hill, MD, 20745. You may also call us at 240 724-7225. Come out and grab a good book, a hot cup of coffee and your favorite old school snacks. Until we hug again!

Yours truly,

T.Styles, President & CEO, The Cartel Publications
www.thecartelpublications.com
www.twitter.com/authortstyles
www.myspace.com/toystyles
www.cartelcafeandbooks.com

Acknowledgements

First and for most I want to thank God for the incredible gift of creativity he has blessed me with. I want to thank my Cartel family for always believing in me and having my back. Special thanks to Toy for always taking time out to listen to me and for the encouraging words; you have truly made a difference in my life. V.J, Tionne, Eyone, and of course Jason I wish you all continued success. Charisse thank you again for believing in this project, you made Poison happen! Davida you did it again! Thanks for the wonderful designs. I can't forget Cee-Cee for always making sure my cup stayed full, lol! Much love to you and Angel! To my Relatives; the Reid, Harris, Hall, Carter, Diggs, Mcneil, and Hines families I send my love. To my blessings from above: Miss Tryniti, (The Diva) and Raevyn (The Angel). I love you girls with all my heart and everything I do is for your benefit. Remember to never let anything or anyone stand in your way speak it and it shall be yours. Nothing is unattainable.

A special thanks to; Ms. Claudette "Dutch" Roberts, I appreciate you so much for stepping up to the plate and helping me with the girls and accepting me as a part of your family. You don't know how much that means to me. I will forever be grateful for your love and kindness. To my Junior Hustlettes: Kyisha, Donnesha, Shay, Denisha, and Andrea. I appreciate you guys for taking time out of your schedules to support my project.

Shout-outs: Dymond, Jab, cousin Pizzle, Meka, and Cornbread(I didn't forget you this time, lol) Monique and Aaron the best God Parents in the world, My spiritual mother Ms. Janet, Sister Reesie, and Pastor Wayne Rudd, thank you so much for being so "real" and not judgmental, I love you for that! Paul from Sunlight Book Source, 9th Street Bookshop, My author friends MQW, Julia Press Simmons, Rich and Sharmina thanks for the support.

Mr. Littles (lol): "When two great minds come together, the world can be conquered." Thank you for being who you are in my life. I appreciate you in so many different ways. I wish you nothing but success and happiness. You're the best!

To all of those who have picked up my books, and supported me throughout my journey... I thank you!

There is more to come! Feel free to e-mail me with oyur thoughts. kdhpresents@yahoo.com or www.myspace.com/author_kdharris.

K.D

Dedication

This book is dedicated to My Fatal...Ms. Cheryl Lyn...The classiest but baddest bitch ever to walk the earth!

Prologue

Eliza Gibbs was disconsolate, and filled with hatred. She looked down at her grandchild with great sadness. Tears filled her eyes as she gazed at the beautiful child that lay before her. She felt that she had lost the good fight and the little life that she had left was rapidly being drained from her weary body. However, the more she watched the fragile child who had been desperately fighting for his life, since his birth over a month ago, gave her hope.

Each breath he took was like new life being breathed into her soul. This child resembled his father, her son who was viciously taken away from her only days ago. She could not dismiss the fact he also shared "angelic" features of the she-devil; who in her mind was responsible for his death. She carefully lifted him from the incubator and held the precious child close to her bosom. She closed her eyes and reminisced of holding her youngest child, some twenty-two years back. *He was a good child. I did the best I could do. I tried to keep him away from the streets.* She thought to herself.

Deep inside she knew she was kidding herself. It was inevitable, that he would choose the street life. It surrounded him from birth, and like the others, it took hold of him no matter how hard she tried to shelter him from it. Sitting back in the wooden rocker she began to rock softly and whispered in his ear.

"Baby…you're all I got. I promise, Mom-Mom will protect you. I lost three people who I loved dearly to these streets. But baby…I promise on my life, I will not lose you."

She opened her eyes and her grandson was staring at her as if he knew what she was talking about. A small smile crept on her face.

"You're safe, baby; she'll never get her hands on you."

She planted a kiss on his tiny forehead and laid him back down. Just as she turned to leave she was troubled by what stood before her.

"*Who* will never get their hands on my son, *Ms. Gibbs?*"

Nyse wore a cunning smile on her face. This was the first time she had seen Ms.Gibbs since the death of Rashawn. She wanted so bad to just curse her out, for what she heard her say. It had been a rumor going around that Ms.Gibbs was petitioning the court to get custody of Lil Kevin. The remark she just made proved the rumor to be true. She knew this wasn't the time but she would most *definitely* have her chance in the near future to put her in her place.

Ms. Gibbs stood there with tears running down her face. She was finally standing face to face with whom she believed was responsible for her son's murder. She didn't understand why Nyse was in good spirits; as if everything was wonderful. *Why is she so happy? Doesn't she care that her sister was just murdered along with her son's father? Why is she still calling this child Lil Kevin? It had been proven that Rashawn was his father!* These questions beleaguered her mind. She wanted to say so much but nothing but whimpers of despair escaped her lips.

Nyse knew that Ms.Gibbs was bothered by her presence. She wanted her to feel like shit. That's the way she used to treat her when she was with Rashawn, and now it was her turn to feel uncomfortable. Nyse put on a façade. She reached over and gently grabbed Ms. Gibbs hand as if she was offering comfort.

"Now, now, Ms. Gibbs there's no use of crying over spilled milk, *especially* when it was… *sour.*"

She kissed Ms. Gibbs on the side of her cheek and made her way down to her son.

"He's getting so big, and looking more and more like

Rashawn…too bad he'll never know he *existed*. I promise you Kevin and I will do a great job of raising him…Who knows maybe one day will even tell him about you." She said in a teasing manner.

Ms. Gibbs couldn't take it anymore, she had heard enough. She ran out of the N.I.C.U into the hallway gasping for air. She held her mouth attempting to cover her cries. She had a gut feeling that Nyse played a big part in her son's death. But how could she get the proof. The cops ruled her out as a suspect almost immediately. She had a strong alibi. When the cops went to look for her, they found her at the hospital. From what they gathered she was there the entire time. That didn't stop her suspicions. If she physically didn't do it, she had it set up.

The look on Nyse's face as she taunted her played over in her mind. Something had to be done. There was no way she could allow her to get away with murder, or raise her grandchild. She hurried down the hall and reached into her pocket to retrieve her cell phone. She dialed a number she vowed to never use again unless she was in dire need. This was definitely the time to use it.

POISON
TWO
A FATAL ATTRACTION

CHAPTER I

A dark cloud hovered over the city of Wilmington, Delaware this Tuesday. Today was the day Katina Nyse and Rashawn Gibbs would be laid to rest. The streets were filled with mourners, as well with those who secretly believed justice had finally been served. The whole tri-state area had been in an uproar since the senseless murders of Rashawn, Kat, and Spinx occurred. Rashawn was a major player in the game, and his death affected many people. No one knew whom to blame so everyone was a suspect. More violence took place as a form of retaliation, but none of them were as important as the "Triangle Murders" or "The Demise of the Monarchs" as some would call it.

The streets were lined with state, city and county police, along with news crews, city officials who were trying to earn a few cool points before election time, ministers who were trying to get the young people to get saved, those who just wanted to be seen, and thousands of spectators. You would have thought it was the Annual Wilmington Jaycee's Christmas Parade about to start. Although there would be a processional; it would not be one of happiness and good cheer. Family and friends who were mourning the death of "Queen Kat and King Rashawn" would lead this procession.

There were rumors out that when their bodies were found. They were laid together on the bed with *Burger King* Crowns, and red sheets tied around their necks like cloaks. Above their heads on the wall written in their blood was *"Behold the Clown Queen and King"*.

K.D. Harris   1

The Westside clique took that as blatant disrespect. That's why they decided that they were going to go out in style like true *Royalty*.

The procession was due to start a 10am from Rashawn's mother's house on 8th and Scott Street, they would travel to a New Church called, The Cathedral of Hope that was located on 27th and Market St. That is the only place that was big enough to hold a crowd of this capacity. There was a huge visual with teddy bears, candles, and pictures of the deceased with friends at the corner of the Gibb's home. A large crowd of people wearing R.I.P t-shirts gathered at the site to pay their respects and follow behind the vehicles as they made their way to the church.

Six white stretch Navigators that were to be filled with immediate family and close friends had just pulled up. The spectators watched in awe as a glass chariot trimmed in platinum drawn by 2 pure white stallions, came up from the side and took its place in front of the cars. Inside you could see 2 identical white and platinum coffins, which carried the bodies of the deceased. It was rumored that the caskets had glass bulletproof tops in case someone wanted to try and act weak at the funeral.

The site of the caskets started an outburst of cries. The hustla's who usually wouldn't show an inch of emotion broke down at the site of the chariot. Different females who had a thing for Rashawn tried to make a dash towards the chariot, hoping to get one last look up close. Their dreams where shattered quickly. The family made sure there was tight security for the deceased.

The crowd was filled with mixed emotions, some embraced and prayed with each other, others talked about the good times, and then there where the ones who were just angry, while others could really care less. They were just there to gossip and hang out because they knew everybody who was anybody would be there.

Moments later the door to The Gibbs' home opened. Everyone fell silent. The first out was Ms. Gibbs, dressed in the traditional black dress, followed by Nyse's mother, Ketara Nyse, followed by her son Nelson. People whispered when they saw Nelson. It was

2

rumored that he was going to be the new nigga in charge. Rashawn and Kat had a will drawn up and it was said that if anything ever happened to them, all of their assets would be left to Nelson. That left a lot of niggas swole.

They boarded the first truck, while other family and close friends boarded the remaining trucks. Everyone watched closely looking for the one person whose name could not stay off their lips, "Nyse". But to their surprise she never came out of the house.

"Where's Nyse, I know she ain't skippin' out on her sisters funeral..." said a young girl with a baby on her hip wearing a R.I.P T-shirt with a picture of Kat and Rashawn.

Another girl sporting the same shirt a few feet over said. "Hmmmph, I heard she bounced out of town."

Another girl who stood behind the chick with the baby was like, "No, she still around. I heard from a reliable source that she on that shit. They said she be on 6th and Washington coppin' syrup and pills." She said convincingly.

"Whaaa-at!" said the girls in unison.

"Yeah, I guess that's what happens when you can't handle the whole world wishing death on you." she said half jokingly.

• •

Nyse sat silently next to Kevin as they circled 26th street in search of a parking spot. She had secretly dreaded the coming of this day. Deep inside she was slowly falling apart. This would be the last time she would see her beloved sister. The picture of the bullet piercing her skull would play over, and over in her mind daily. Even though the world thought otherwise, she truly loved Kat. She didn't want her to die. Yeah, she made her mad, and sometimes she thought she hated her. But they shared the same blood, came from the same loins, birthed from the same womb. She was her sister.

Now she was gone...because of some *psycho jealous bitch*,

who had betrayed both of them. Nyse felt a lump form in her throat. *Get it together Nyse. Play your part. Never let them see your true intentions.* She reminded herself. There was not one day that went by that she did not contemplate vengeance. Nyse felt as if she had nothing to lose now. She was numb and her family had forsaken her. Her best friend Kee left her when she needed her most, and then there was Ms. Gibbs. She was plotting to take the only person she had any love for away. Nyse had a plan for them all. They would all wish they had done right by her especially that bitch Fatal.

Kevin finally found a spot not far from Price's Park. They would only need to walk a few blocks before they reached the church. They walked in silence hand in hand until they reached the double glass stained doors of the church. Kevin ran his hand on the side of her cheek. Even though her feelings for him weren't as strong as they were two weeks ago, she couldn't help but notice how fine he looked in his Charcoal Armani suit.

"You ready baby?"

Nyse smiled taking a deep breath for strength.

"Yeah, I'm good."

They walked in hand in hand inside the building through a thick crowd of spectators. Nyse refused to make eye contact with anyone in the crowd. She heard whispers and smart remarks, but kept it moving. Even though she badly wanted to respond this was neither the time nor the place. She needed to make peace with Kat in her own way. The ushers opened the doors to the sanctuary for them. Even though there was no room left to sit they were still given the opportunity to view the bodies.

Nyse was amazed at how beautiful the sanctuary was. Poster size pictures of Rashawn and Kat hung from the ceiling decorated with sequins, and handmade angels. There was an arch adorned with white roses, pink and green carnations, that spelled out *Together Forever*. It was absolutely breathtaking. It looked more like a wedding ceremony than a funeral.

All eyes were on her as she and Kevin walked down the aisle.

4

Unlike in the hallway, Nyse held her head high, and waved and smiled to the onlookers like she was Miss America and was about to receive her crown. The fact was she did look like a beauty Queen. She was dressed in a Peach Linen Dior Sleeveless Dress, which complemented her body. Her long black hair, which she wore, curled, fell loosely against her mid shoulders. If it wasn't for the black hair and fair skin you would have thought it was Kat herself gliding down the aisle. As she came closer to the caskets she felt her stomach begin to knot up.

Once they made it to the last pew Nyse looked to her right and noticed her mother. They made eye contact for a brief second. Bitterness consumed her mother's face. Nyse returned a smug look as well. She wasn't surprised at her reaction. Ketara made it clear in her actions that she was dead to her, and she was fine with it.

Nyse watched on as Kevin went up to Rashawn's casket. He threw up the Westside sign, and nodded his head in acknowledgement. He went over to Kat and stood there for a moment said a few words and walked back towards Nyse who was now trembling.

"You need me to walk you up there?" he whispered.

Nyse shook her head calmly. "I'm cool, I got this."

She slowly made her way to Kat's body. Taking a deep breath she closed her eyes and ran her hand over top of the glass. When she opened them she didn't see Kat. She saw an angel, at least that's what she looked like. Kat had on a white Versace halter style evening gown, adorned with crystals, and beautiful ivory beads. She wore a tiara that had enough bling to light up the darkness that would be her home for an eternity.

A single tear dropped from her eye. *Stay strong Nyse.* She reminded herself again. It was all so overwhelming. The dress reminded her of the day her and Kat went to Atlantic City. She picked it out for her. She remembered arguing with her because Kat told her it wasn't traditional enough. She never knew that Kat went back to get it. There was so much she wanted to say. There was a guy from the funeral home standing next to the casket. She beckoned him over to her.

"How can I help you, ma'am?" He was an older gentleman and looked to be in his mid 40's.

"Could you please open the top?" He looked at Nyse oddly.

"I have to ask the parents, first ma'am."

He went over to her mother and told them her request. Ketara flat out said no, but Nelson tried to reason with her. After a few minutes of deliberation; Nelson stood by Nyse while the man lifted the top. At this point everyone began to talk amongst themselves, wondering what was about to happen. Once the top was lifted she touched her sister's hands, which were stiff and cold. She then ran her hands over the dress and grinned. She leaned over and whispered in her ear, as if she could hear.

"I thought you didn't like this dress, hussy. I told you it would be pretty on you didn't I?" She waited for a moment like there would be a response. "I promise I will make them all pay. I love you, Katty."

She kissed her sister's forehead in the same spot the bullet hit, which was now undetectable. She stood there until the top was lowered again. She looked at her one last time, but this time she noticed something, she had never noticed before. Her reflection from the glass was identical to the face that lied beneath it. She never thought she looked like her sister, but looking at Kat was like looking in the mirror. For the first time in her life she felt a bond with her sister.

She turned to walk back down the aisle towards Kevin, but was stopped by her brother Nelson. He embraced her and whispered.

"Don't disrespect my people's like that. You need to show him some love. He did bless you wit' a seed. People are watching and I can't let you play him out like that."

Nyse's tears dried up instantly. She laughed at her brothers' request. *Is this lil nigga serious? Show him love, yeah right!* She thought. They were still embracing each other when Nyse looked up in his eyes. He stared at her hard with assurance that he meant everything he just said. Nelson was no longer the scrawny little 14-year-old that used to follow Rashawn foot to foot. He had grown into a young man. Who was next in line to take over Rashawn's empire?

6

She gently broke away and made her way to Rashawn's casket. From what she could see he looked really like himself. He wore a white Versace suit that matched Kat's dress and a crown on his head also. Nyse looked around and noticed all eyes were on her. She even caught Ms. Gibbs watching her like a hawk. A devilish grin spread across her face.

She hurried and lifted the top to his casket, and hocked a glob of thick spit right in his face. The crowd cried out in rage. Nyse blew a kiss at Ms. Gibbs before she ran out the side door to escape her fate. Ms. Gibbs ran to her sons casket and began to wipe his face, which smeared the heavy makeup and caused a distorted look. Nelson stood in the same spot where Nyse left him in disbelief. He felt as if his heart had been snatched from his chest. He couldn't believe how vile his sister had become. All the love he had for her was null and void. Rashawn was like a big brother/father to him and she had totally disrespected him. Hate pumped through his body. She was just like any other nigga on the street to him now, and he promised that she would be dealt with for her actions.

CHAPTER 2

Weak ass Niggas

"Why...God why did you take him away! He's all I got...he's all I got...Why!"

Fae watched from the third row trying to hide her laughter as the pallbearers tried their hardest to pry Kita off of Spinx's corpse. Her grip on him was so tight that when they pulled her, she damn near pulled him along with her straight out of the coffin. Fae wasn't the only one who found Kita's performance hilarious. Spinx's own mother hid her laughter behind the program she pretended to be reading.

Braxton "Spinx" Hayes funeral was held at the Congo Funeral home. It was nothing spectacular at all. No parade, no R.I.P t-shirts, just a few of his faithful fuck buddies, and his *wife* Sakita Hayes. She knew Spinx would not have wanted to go out like this, wearing a cheap navy Value City suit with Payless pleather shoes. He wasn't even going to have a proper burial. He was being cremated. Ms. Nett was the beneficiary on the insurance, which was for $100,000. From the looks of it his service was probably under $5000 and she knew she was wrong for that.

None of his boys from the hills was there. Fae wasn't surprised about the turnout. She knew Spinx's days were numbered so she didn't feel bad about handling him at all. A few weeks ago the truth had finally come out about Braxton's early release from prison. The infamous "Spinx" turned pussy and couldn't handle being in jail, so he decided to be a bitch and become a snitch for the police.

He ran tape on all of his "boys", including his best friend Bo, who was now looking at a possible 20 years. His job was to set up Rashawn, he knew Nyse was messing with him so he figured he could use the hold he had on her to complete his task. However, the joke was on him. Nyse and her scheming self totally flipped it on him. She knew Spinx couldn't resist her, and totally used his weakness to her advantage. His enthrallment of chasing young pussy caused his death.

Fae looked down at her diamond embedded Tiffany's watch, which read 12:10pm. She wondered what was going on over at Rashawn's funeral across town. She would have been there but for the first time in her life guilt had over taken her. Although she had done it many times with others, and was doing it now with Spinx, she just couldn't bring herself to sit up in Rashawn's funeral, knowing she was responsible for his fatality.

Deep down inside Fae truly loved Rashawn. They had been through so much together while growing up. He knew her deepest darkest secrets and vice versa. He was her first in many ways, from a kiss, to sex, to stick-ups, and murder. Killing him was like committing suicide to half of her life. She fought inwardly with herself since that fatal night. She had to do it she would tell herself. *He was getting soft, by letting that bitch run over him. She plotted murder against him not once but twice; and he was letting her get away with it.* In her mind she saved him from himself.

Fae felt a headache coming on. She opened her black Prada clutch bag and pulled out her Imitrex prescription. She opened it up and popped a pill. She had been having serious migraines for the last few days. She looked around to see if anyone else was coming because she was tired and wanted this to be over. The place was still empty. Kita had finally made it back to her seat. The speaker read his eulogy and spoke a few words about Spinx and then there was an alter call and it was finally over.

● ●

"Nyse, you know that was some real childish shit you just did!" Kevin snapped. He was hot with Nyse for her actions at the funeral. "What the fuck is wrong wit' you? Don't you even think? There was a million fuckin' cops in there and you going to go and spit in that dead niggas face! Don't you think they gonna question that shit?"

Kevin slammed the door to his hotel suite and followed Nyse into the bedroom area. These last couple of days he had been thrown off by her demeanor. One minute she was all loving towards him and the next she was on some fuck you shit. He knew she was going through a lot, her mom cut her off, she lost her sister, and her son's health still wasn't quite right. She had a shot with being all right with her brother until she pulled that stunt at the funeral.

Nyse sat on the bed and kicked off her shoes not paying Kevin any mind. Kevin was truly getting on her nerves. Ever since the night the murders took place he had been on some domineering bullshit. He tried to map out her every move, tell her how she should *feel,* where she should live, how she should answer questions if anyone asked. *Didn't that motherfucka know that I'm the one who masterminded this whole shit? I don't need coaching from his ass I got this under control.* She would say to herself. She wanted so bad to be able to express her *true* feelings, but she knew now was not the time. She knew in order for the plan to work she had to play nice; and she hated playing nice.

She walked over to him and seductively wrapped her arms around his neck. She stood on her tippy toes and planted a kiss on his lips. "Baby, I'm sorry. You know I'm impulsive and shit. Nelson was kicking all this respect shit, and how I needed to show that nigga grat-itude, and you know…looking at that sick motherfucka just bought back all types of memories and I just snapped."

Kevin didn't want to, but he began to feel sorry for Nyse. He knew that she blamed Rashawn for her sister's death. Honestly he didn't think she owed him shit, especially respect. But he knew they

10

had a plan and being on her brother's good side was a part of it.

He ran his fingers through her silky locks of curls and held her closely. He held on to her tightly as if someone was attempting to snatch her away. He truly loved Nyse, regardless of the fact that she was "damaged goods." He didn't blame her for her actions. He blamed Spinx, Rashawn and her family. In his mind they were the ones who turned her into the person she had become. Sadly just like the others Kevin was blinded by her beauty, and manipulative, poisoned ways. Nyse knew this and just like the others she would use his weakness to her advantage.

CHAPTER 3

Don't Want No Short Man

Three long days had passed since the funerals. Kevin held Nyse captive in his suite going over their game plan. At this point, she could recite his speech frontward and backwards and she was tired of hearing it. Not only was she tired of his mouth, she was sick of the nigga's weak ass sex game he was laying down around the clock. Although she had only been with two men prior to him, he was indeed the *worst*. Kevin had a sickness she called "little man's syndrome". Meaning his dick was extremely too small. She remembered the first night they had sex, it was the day after everything went down. She was grieving over the lost of her sister, her mother's rejection, and so much more. They were in her apartment on the couch and he held her in his arms.

"It's gonna be aight' you got me, Lil Kev and *Fae*. You don't need anybody else." He kissed her softly on her cheek and wiped her tears away.

Nyse wanted desperately to believe him, and she did until he said the name that was like poison to her ears, *Fae*. She hated her and in no way shape or form was she ever going to trust her.

"I love you Nalyse and we will be a family. When all of this is over and Lil Kev is well enough, we leaving this place and never looking back...I promise."

His words soothed her soul for the moment. She needed to feel wanted, and loved. That's all she ever wanted, nothing more, but for some reason people found it hard to give that to her. Now she had this gorgeous, strong man who she wanted to believe had her best interest at heart, but due to certain circumstances, she realized she could never trust him.

She laid her head on his chest as he began to caress her body and explore places he hadn't visited on her before. His touch felt heavenly and she felt herself slipping into an eccentric ecstasy. She lay back on the couch and watched as he removed her pants and placed soft kisses in between her thighs, and down her legs, even to her feet. He massaged her whole body and whispered sweet words to her. For a moment all of her issues where desolate, all that mattered was them at that moment.

"Promise you'll never leave me." she moaned as he gently massaged her clit. Kevin sucked gently on her neck and chest leaving *love bites*.

"I promise you, baby, I'll never leave you…it's till *death* do us part."

Nyse moaned deeply the words "till death do us part" which heightened her arousal, and at this point she needed to feel him inside her. The stimulation without *penetration* was all good for a moment, but she was the type of chick who needed to be *dicked* down properly.

Kevin slid his pants down as she pulled his Eddie Bauer Rugby shirt over his head exposing his muscular chest. She began to nibble on his erect nipples as he placed her legs over his shoulders. He rubbed the head against her clit, which made her shudder with excitement. She had waited for this for over a year and it was finally about to go down. Kevin thrust his body against hers and began to pump vigorously. Nyse could feel and hear his balls slapping against her ass, but for some reason she didn't feel him inside of her walls. He picked up the pace and began to grind deeply into her, as he moaned and cried out her name. Moments later he collapsed on her chest and held her tightly. "You okay, baby." He asked.

Nyse had a perplexed look on her face. *I know this nigga ain't just bust off from humping. He ain't even get in the pussy.* She placed her hand between her legs and felt the stickiness all around her open-

K.D. Harris   13

ing. Then she placed her hand on his dick. The head was a nice size but when she ran her hand over it she soon met the base.

Frustration overcame her immediately. *No...this can't be!* She thought. Not only was Kevin a minuteman, that nigga possessed a handicap. He was a victim of "Little Man Syndrome". It was thick but it was no longer than her middle finger. Nyse felt sick immediately. She pushed him off of her and ran to the bathroom where she cried herself to sleep.

The next morning he was feeling some type of way. Just to save his ego she gave him some lame excuse about feeling crazy about sexing him in Rashawn's apartment. She lied to him and told him that it was the best sex she ever had, so now that nigga felt like superman and was hitting her off ever chance they got. She tried to get him to give her some head, but that nigga ain't believe in oral sex. He just wanted to do it missionary style, since his little dick would fall out in any other position. So she was screwed when it came to getting good sex, literally.

• •

Nyse was in the bathroom brushing her hair into a ponytail, when she heard a knock at the door. Kevin was about to head out to handle some business, and she was about to go to her apartment to continue packing up her things. She and Kevin were moving to a row home on Van Buren Ave. in North Wilmington. It was cute but she just wasn't trying to be in the city like that. He said it was only temporary and she agreed although she still wasn't feeling it too tough. She heard the door open and then shut. She heard him talking in a hush tone, she moved closer to the door to try and hear the conversation. But nothing was heard.

Holding her hair in place, she placed each strand into a Scrunchy ponytail holder and exited the bathroom. She went over to the closet and slipped on her brown coach sandals and matching pocketbook. She opened the door that led into the living room area

14

and was greeted by a phony smile.

"Hello Nalyse, how are you this afternoon?" Fae said cordially.

She sat next to Kevin with her legs crossed wearing an Yves Saint Laurent, powder blue sundress that flowed elegantly to her ankles. She had on a hot pair of silver strap up sandals. Her flawless bronze skin was sun kissed, causing her skin to have a radiant glow. Her hair was weaved up in a Chinese ponytail. Nyse couldn't stand the site of her, but had to admit she was definitely a bad bitch. From her dress game, to her a character, she was a force to be reckoned with. She knew she had her work cut out for her, but she was up for the challenge.

Nyse smiled and extended out her arms. Fae returned the smile and strutted over to her and gave her a hug. "You look good. Where have you been, lady?" Nyse inquired. Fae sat back down next to Kevin and crossed her legs.

"Well let's see, after Braxton's funeral, I decided to get away for a while, you know and clear my mind. So much shit is going on, and you know a bitch just needed some time to herself. So, I went to Miami, and enjoyed the beaches and did some shopping."

Nyse wanted to ask Fae a million questions about Spinx's funeral, like who was there, what he had on, how did Ms. Nett take it. But she decided against it. Kevin would feel some type of way about her interest if she did. Most likely, he'd probably accuse her of still having some type of feelings for him. Nyse stood up and prepared to leave. Fae studied her for a moment and said.

"How was Tina's funeral?" Nyse stopped in her tracks. She wanted to cuss Fae out, that bitch didn't deserve to speak her sister's name. She took a deep breath and calmed down before she answered.

"It was beautiful, *she* looked beautiful, and she wore her Versace wedding dress, the one I picked out for her to wear for her and *Rashawn's wedding*. She looked like and Angel in it, and Congo made her face *flawless*, you would have never guessed that the bullet hole *you* inflicted was ever there?"

Fae looked at Kevin as if to say you better get this bitch before I fuck her up. She knew Nyse was being cynical. Fae had thought everything was cool between them, but after making that remark, she wasn't sure if she did the right thing by letting that bitch live. *What if she went to the police*? It's not like she had any care when it came to the street code, Nyse ain't give a fuck and that's why Fae halfway liked her. She saw herself in Nyse, and wanted to take her on as some sort of protégé. But that couldn't happen if she kept talking reckless like that.

Kevin felt the tension in the air and spoke up before anything popped off. He loved Fae like a sister but he loved Nyse like a wife. She was his future. He refused to let Fae take that away from him as she did with so many others in the past. He knew she also had a lot of issue's from the pain her mother inflicted. She had her revenge, he was there to witness it, but now it was time for her to move on.

"The funeral was alright. They did have it set up all Hollywood in shit. But let me tell you 'bout what your girl did, she was on some ole' rowdy type shit. How bout' she spit in homeboy's face! Nelson was 'bout to straight lace kill her ass, or at least attempt to, if she ain't run out the fuckin' side door!" Kevin said trying to make a joke out of Nyse's disrespect.

Nyse laughed along with him, while reading Fae's expressions. There wasn't a trace of a smile on Fae's face; as a matter of fact she wore a grimacing look. She knew hearing that bit of news didn't sit well with her at all. Nyse tried to control her laughter.

"Fae, you ok *babe*?" Nyse asked. Fae smiled weakly.

"I'm straight, but you out of control, Nyse. That was classic right there. Some, *I'll spit on your grave shit*…but you know you fucked up. There's no way that we can get in with Nelson after that stunt."

"You need to talk to your brother about that, you know he always has plan A, B, and C and I'm tired of hearing it. So I'ma let him bore you to death wit' the details." She said as she grabbed her pocketbook off the table.

16

She went over to Kevin and kissed him deeply in his mouth putting on a show for Fae. She knew she really didn't approve of their relationship. Kevin had told her that one day when they were in a heated discussion. She gave Fae *a play-play hug* and was out the door.

As she was closing it she heard Fae say, "That bitch is a fucking problem, Kevin! You need to get her ass in check for she has us all caught the fuck up!"

Nyse laughed to herself. She knew she had a point, she *was* a fucking problem, and there was nothing they could do about it.

CHAPTER 4

What Could Be Worse?

The apartment reeked of shit and piss. Debris was scattered through out the floor. Her clothes were cut up and stained with bleach. One of her brass and onyx dining room chairs rested in the middle of her 52-inch screen television. The salmon pink Italian leather furniture was now slashed, and smeared with human feces. All of her and Rashawn's jewels, furs, and anything that had any value to it, were all gone. The only things untouched were Lil Kevin's possessions.

Nyse sat on her kitchen counter swinging her legs like a little kid while the two officers took a report of the incident. When she first came home and found her door slightly ajar, she was cautious before entering. She called the cops on her cell phone and told them her home had been invaded and she thought the perpetrators were still there. The operator informed her that a unit was on its way and for her not to go inside until they arrived. She sat in her truck until she heard the sirens in the background.

A male and female officer came out of the vehicle and escorted her into the apartment. Once they were at the door they both drew their weapons and told her to stay outside until all was clear. A few minutes later, the female officer, who reminded her of the female wrestler China, came to the door.

"Everything is clear, but I don't think you'll like what you're about to see." She said in a *mannish* voice. She sounded like she had a pile of shit lounged in her throat.

Nyse walked through the door and felt faint when she smelled the odor, and saw the hell hole that was once her pride and joy. The male officer had a pitiful look on his face.

"Young lady, do you know who would want to do something like this to you? Are you in any type of danger that we should know about?" The officer felt sorry for her.

He thought she was probably in an abusive relationship, and this was the work of her deranged boyfriend. He had seen cases like this many times involving young girls who fell in love with drug dealers and what they could offer them only to end up being their punching bags. But as he looked Nyse over, he didn't see any visible marks on her. He believed that if she were here when this took place, he would be discovering her dead body.

Nyse shook her head no.

"Well I need you to make a list of anything that may be missing, but before we do that I need to get your name."

"Nalyse Lynae Nyse, I was born 8/21/76." The female cop walked over to her when she heard her name.

"Did you say your last name was Nyse, as in Katina Nyse, who was murdered a couple weeks ago?" The male cop looked at his partner in confusion. Nyse rolled her eyes and caught and instant attitude.

"Yeah…my name is Nyse, Katina was my sister! But what the fuck does that have to do with anything? I was violated and someone fucking vandalized my shit. This ain't got shit to do with her!" She was pissed off.

The fake ass Cagney and Lacey cop was getting on her last nerve. The cop pulled her partner aside. "Do you know that this is the young lady that was in middle of that whole mess? The Gibbs guy is the father of her child, who was engaged to her sister, and she's the ex-girlfriend of that Spinx character. She's full of drama, and has many enemies, anyone could have done this to her." She looked over at Nyse and rolled her eyes and whispered. "The little bitch probably deserved it!"

She didn't think Nyse heard her.

"Fuck you too, you, buff bitch!" she said sarcastically. "What are you a fucking transvestite? You manly looking, bitch!"

The cop was about to jump in her face but was stopped by her partner. He handed Nyse the pad and pen. "That's enough young lady, we're here to help you, now you need to calm down before you get yourself in trouble." He said trying to show some authority.

The truth was he always thought the same thing about his partner, but never said it. So he found her comments quite humorous, and Nyse quite beautiful. He felt guilty for even looking at her; he was a married man with a family. Nyse playfully took the pad and pen and took inventory of her belongings.

While the female cop took pictures to be added to their report, her partner made his way over to the kitchen to talk with Nyse. "I have all of your information and if you need *anything* don't hesitate to call me." He handed her his card, which read Officer Corey Hamilton. She smiled charmingly.

"Are you sure about that officer Hamilton? At this point in my life I tend to be a *very* needy person." She said in a sexy voice.

Corey felt his manhood awaken immediately. He would love to fulfill every one of her needs, and more if he was given the chance. Nyse looked down and noticed the bulged in his pants and got excited herself. He may be useful in more than one way she thought. He was handsome, he had that "distinguished gentlemen look", like Denzel Washington. She slid off the counter and purposely brushed her ass against his dick as she bent over to tie the laces on her Air Max's. His partner watched the little freak show that was happening before her eyes in disgust.

"Ok, we're done here. Let's go, Corey." She said with an attitude.

Corey hurried out the door behind his partner, before leaving he whispered. "Call me!" Nyse tucked the card in her bra. She would definitely be putting his number to use.

Later that evening Nyse went to the hospital to check on her son. Everything was all good. He was now 4lbs 3oz, and taking an ounce at a time during feedings. The doctor informed her that if he kept this up he would be home within the next couple of weeks. Hearing that news was like music to her ears. She couldn't wait to finally have her son home with her.

After her talk with the doctor she wanted to get home to tell Kevin the good news. On her way out she was stopped by this geeky white guy, who had an envelope in his hands. "Excuse me, are you Nalyse Nyse?" Nyse rolled her eyes.

"No, my name is Nalyse pronounced *Nah-Leese*, not no damn Nalis." She said disgusted.

The man said sarcastically, "Well *Nalyse*, you have been served!" and he walked away.

What the fuck...served? She opened the envelope and it was a petition for full custody. The petitioner was no other than Eliza Gibbs. She read further down. She made accusations of Nalyse not being a stable mother, that she was involved with drug dealers, and all other types of shit. There was even a statement attached from Nyse's own mother that she wasn't fit.

These bitches are ganging up on me? She thought. Tears filled her eyes at the thought of her mother's betrayal. She couldn't believe that her mother hated her so much that she would take the only person who meant the world to her away. She tucked the papers in her bag and stormed out of the hospital. She picked up her cell phone and called Jael's Beauty Salon.

"Jael's Caree speaking."

"Hey Ree! It's Nyse I need a favor."

"Hey girl, how are you? Me and the twins been so worried about you. What's up?"

"Meet me at the Travelodge on New Castle ave, around 10 tonight and bring the twins with you. We need to handle something."

Caree was a little hesitant at first. She knew that Nyse and her had an off and on relationship, mostly due to Nyse's insecurity. But she knew her girl needed her so she was going to come through, she just hoped she wasn't the one she needed to be handled.

CHAPTER 5

The Bitch Ain't Playin'

Nyse paced the floors in the motel room waiting for her girls to get there. It was now 10:15 and they still arrived. Her head was pounding as she thought about today's events. The good news she received concerning her son was now on the back burner. Revenge consumed her mind. She was tired of playing with these people, and they needed to be dealt with. Her cell phone rang off the hook. She checked the number and it was Kevin calling for the thousandth time. She wasn't in the mood to deal with him at the moment. She had her own shit to handle. *He don't want anything anyway* she thought. That cell phone had been more of a problem than a blessing. That was just his way of keeping tabs on her, and it was starting to work her nerve. Five minutes later there was laughter and a knock at her door. Nyse ran over to the door and snatched the door open.

"Damn, Bitches, it's about fucking time you got here. I thought I said to be here at 10 o'clock. What are you...the fuck retarded? You can't tell time or something?" The girls got quiet and filed into the room. Muff was the first to speak.

"Is that how you greet a mother fucka, when you the one who *needs* them? You called looking for us, if I'm not mistaken." Muff always stood her ground.

Nyse never intimidated her, even after the rumors that floated around about her setting up those murders. Muff knew Nyse for *real*. Nyse wasn't a fighter and she damn sure wasn't going to do shit to them. Her brother was an OG, out the hills and had many connections. So if Nyse wanted to act weak, all she had to do was say the word, and she would be handled. But Muff loved Nyse and doubted it would ever come to that. Buff and Caree looked on hoping that shit wasn't about to get out of hand. Caree didn't know whose side to jump in if it did. She already knew Buff would be down with her sister.

Nyse looked Muff up and down trying to figure her out. She hoped she wasn't serious, because she had love for her and would hate to have to add her ass to the list of havoc. Nyse playfully pushed her.

"Fuck you bitch, look seriously I need y'all."

She pulled the papers out of her bag and handed it to her. Muff read it over and a serious look came on her face. "Damn babe, that's fucked up. How you want to handle this?" Those were the words Nyse wanted to hear.

They all sat around that night laughing and joking about the past and more importantly masterminding a plan that would keep Lil Kevin in Nyse's custody forever.

• •

Two weeks had passed since Nyse received her court papers. Lil' Kevin was being released in two days. He had finally gotten his weight to 5lbs 7oz and was eating 2 oz or sometimes more at his feedings. Things between her and Kevin were going downhill too. Since they moved to the city, Kevin had started to act more like her father, than her man and it was driving her nuts. The fact that Fatal was at their crib damn near everyday didn't help either. She felt like she was being smothered, and needed some air. So, she decided to take Officer Corey up oh his offer and for the last week he had been her life support system, breathing new life into her. He fulfilled her every need, and made her feel like the woman she was, at least in the bedroom. Nyse found out that Corey was married, after the first night they had sex. He had just got finished dicking her down righteously for the third time. She was lying on the bed awaiting round four.

"Nalyse, baby can you get me a rag with a little soap on it, so I can wash up?" She sat up in the bed with a confused look on her face.

"Baby, you leaving me already?" She looked at her DKNY watch.

"It's only 11:30, why can't you stay the night and go to work from here?" she whined.

Corey buttoned his shirt and went to the bathroom to retrieve the rag himself. He should have known this was going to happen. Maybe he should have been honest with her before they fucked. That way she could have made her own decision about getting involved with him. He looked back at her beautiful naked body and quickly changed his mind. There was no way he could have told her before he got a taste of that delicious pussy.

His dick began to rise again at the thought of what just took place. That young girl had put it on his 38-year-old body. But the way she was screaming and carrying on, he knew he had put it on her as well. He sat on the edge of the bed as he wiped himself off.

"I don't know how to tell you this and maybe I should have told you this before we did anything." He sighed and caressed the side of her face. "Baby, I'm married, but I'm not happy. I'm just there because...I don't know. I guess I feel sorry for her. She can't have kids."

Nyse sat looking straight ahead with a blank look on her face. She listened to him babble on and on. She knew it was all bullshit. She didn't want him to leave his wife. She kind of figured he was married anyway. She just wanted him to treat her equally. She refused to be anyone's side chick again. She wanted every benefit his wife received if not more.

Nyse knew he was feeling her, that's why she put it on him the way she did. She sucked that man from head to toe and he was blown away by her sex game, but she had to admit he was no slouch either.

He had her "girl" on swole. She knew she was going to have to sit in a tub of vinegar before she went back home to Kevin. She covered herself up with the sheets and put on a sad look.

"I don't think this is going to work. I think you're a great guy and you make me feel wonderful. I can see myself easily falling in love with you. But, you're a married man, with a career, and I'm just some young pussy that don't really mean shit to you. I've been hurt beyond measure in the past and my life is complicated. I have a son who was pre-mature and he needs me to have a level head. I can't get mixed up with you and end up depressed, and crying over a man who can't even spend the night with me. "

Nyse whipped up some tears, and began to cry softly. She pulled the cover over her head to hide the embarrassment. Corey's heart melted immediately. He knew just what she was talking about. He heard about her situation around the station. A lot of his colleagues thought she was somehow responsible for the deaths, but they couldn't find any concrete evidence besides that she was involved with all three victims closely. He felt bad for her, and blamed her parents for her fate. He wouldn't tell anyone this, but if she did have anything to do with the murders he didn't blame her one bit for committing them. He didn't want to see her hurt she been through enough. He thought about it for a moment. He unbuttoned his shirt and climbed back in the bed holding her in his arms.

"Baby, I can't leave you like this. I promise you we will make this work somehow." Nyse sniffled and laid her head on his chest and beamed on the inside. *Another victory won.*

• •

Caree sat at the desk scheduling appointments at Jael's hair salon. Two weeks had passed since the meeting with Nyse. Today was the day the plan was to go down. She was very nervous about the details. She didn't want this to fall back on her in any way. She was due to start Shaw University this fall, and she wasn't trying to have

26

this bullshit stop her plans.

Caree looked in her fake Gucci bag that she had purchased from a street vendor earlier that day and pulled out a stick of juicy fruit. She put the gum in her mouth and began to chew until her mouth got all juicy. When she lifted her head up she almost choked on her saliva. Coughing and gagging, she held her finger up as if to say hold on. She took a gulp of the Deer Park Spring water she had on her desk, and took a breath. "Excuse, me I'm sorry, good afternoon how can I help you?"

The woman looked at her sharply. "You don't know who I am by now? It's been what…2 months and I've been coming the same time every Thursday and you still don't know my name? Please tell Jael I'm here." She said sternly.

Caree got up from the desk and walked to the back of the shop. Jael was sitting at his station gossiping and plucking his eyebrows. "Jae your two o'clock is here." She said flatly.

He rolled his eyes and pretended to stick his finger down his throat. "Old trout! Her breath smell like Pall Mall's. She lucky she tip good or I would have been told her about herself" he joked causing the other patrons to laugh. "Send her back, baby."

Caree put on a fake smile as she went back to the front. "You can go on back Ms. Gibbs. Jae's waiting for you."

She put the magazine down and pushed past Caree. At that moment Caree was happy that the she was about to get exactly what she deserved. She went to her desk and pulled out her cell phone that Nyse bought for her.

"She's here."

• •

The Wilmington Police department flooded, Jael's Hair Salon. Everyone was in shock at what just went down. Two people dressed in black armed with baseball bats, came in and beat Ms. Gibbs until she was unconscious blood was everywhere. The police questioned

Caree.

"Did you see what they looked like? Were they male or female?" Caree cried holding her swollen jaw.

"I don't know it happened so quick. I was putting the shampoo bottles on the shelf and I felt something hit me in the face. I was in so much pain! It had me in shock. I heard screaming in the back and that's when I called you guys! I don't know! I just don't know what happened. Is she ok?"

"I'm not sure but it doesn't look good." The policeman took her statement and sent her over to the ambulance for treatment.

CHAPTER 6

Demons from the Past

The aroma of French Vanilla scented Glade air freshener mixed with a hint of the finest and most potent chronic in the tri-state area lingered in the atmosphere. Fae lied naked on her back entangled within her lily-white satin sheets watching the blades of her ceiling fan whirl around at high speed. She took a pull off her blunt and inhaled deeply. She felt at one with the blades. All of her life she felt like she was in a high-speed whirlwind. She exhaled slowly letting the smoke seep from her mouth and nostrils. She placed the blunt in the crystal ashtray that sat on her nightstand.

Fae thought about the dreadful hand that life had dealt her. From birth, death surrounded her. Her father was killed in the hospital's lobby, twenty minutes after she was born, by the hands of her mothers' father, who afterwards shot himself. At the tender age of 14 her mother Felicia, gave birth to her. Her 32-year-old father Quentin was by her mother's side. It was said that he loved "Fee", despite her young age. But Fee's father didn't approve of him. So she hid her pregnancy, the whole nine months. When she went into labor the whole family was in shock. Overwhelmed with rage, her father went on a rampage vowing that Quentin would never see the light of day again. The only thing her father left behind for her to cherish was her name Fatalia Edwards…the name he gave her.

Fae'e vision became blurred with tears as she thought about the father she never knew. In her early years, her mother would tell her many stories, and share pictures of him with her. It made her feel like he was still alive, just away on an extended vacation. That all came to an end when Fae turned 11 years old and Sheronda moved in. All talk about Quentin came to an end, the pictures disappeared, and anything that reminded her mother of him was destroyed including Fae.

The phone began to ring allowing Fae to escape her thoughts. She wiped her eyes with the back of her hand drying any tears that were attempting to escape. Still lying on her back, she picked the cordless phone that lay next to her up, and hit the talk button.

"Hello" she said softly.

"*May I speak to Fatalia Edwards?*" Said an unfamiliar female voice.

Fae sighed. She figured it was a telemarketer trying to sell her something, or a bill collector. They were the only ones who called her by her first name.

"Look, I don't owe shit to nobody and I damn sure ain't buying shit so take my name off of ya'll fucking list!" She was about to bang on her until she heard a male's voice call her name.

"*Fatal!*" Paranoia overpowered her psyche. *It can't be!* She thought. "*I'm at the Christiana Hospital's trauma unit. You need to be here...now!*" The phone went dead.

• •

Fae made it to the Christiana Hospital in 10 minutes. She parked her car, in the handicap zone, not caring that it would be a good chance that her car would be towed. She'd rather pay the impound fee, than suffer the consequences she would encounter for being disobedient. She rushed through the revolving doors, and headed to the information desk. A young teenage girl sat behind the desk in front of the computer.

"May I help you, Miss?" she said bubbly.

"Yeah, I need the trauma unit, umm ...someone called me and said I needed to be here." She stammered.

30

The girl looked confused. "Miss, do you have a family member in trauma? Only family can go back there."

Fae's patience was wearing thin. She didn't know why or who, or if anybody was actually hurt. She just knew she had to be there.

"I...I don't know. I got a call from a friend telling me to meet him in the trauma unit. Could you just give me a nametag, and buzz me in? I need to be there!" she tried to keep her composure but she was falling apart. Fae hated not having it together.

"Miss, I can't let you through, if *you* don't *know* who you're even here for. Maybe you should try calling your friend back and he could give you more information. Now if you could excuse me there are more people in line who need assistance." She said smiling.

Fae couldn't take it anymore. If that glass window wasn't there protecting her she would have reached through and choked the life out of her. She clenched her teeth, and moved closer to the window and said loud enough for only the girl to hear.

"Look here you stupid, lil bitch, you're gonna open this fuckin' door if you don't your mother will be visiting you not in trauma, but the fuckin' morgue! Open ...the... fuckin' ...door!"

Fae took a deep breath, and stepped back keeping her eyes glued to the girl who looked like she was about to shit her herself. The door clicked, Fae pulled it open and smiled.

"Thanks, sweetheart!" she said to the now red-faced girl.

Fae ran down the hall until she reached the trauma unit. She busted through the lobby doors scanning the room, for a familiar face. She went up to the front desk and retrieved a clipboard, with a sign in sheet attached. She skimmed down until she saw the name she was looking for. Her heart felt like it stopped. *He's here...he's really back!* She placed it down on the counter. Backing away from the counter she stumbled and almost fell. Before she hit the ground she felt strong arms pulling her up. Their eyes met for the first time in seven years.

"Eric, I...I can't believe it's you."

Fae didn't know what to expect so much had changed since he'd been gone. She studied his face and noticed he was upset. Then it hit her. *Rashawn*.

"Don't tell me you just finding out about him, I would have thought your mother, or someone would have told you. I would have told you but I didn't have any way to contact you."

He cut her off. "I knew 'bout Ra. That's not why I called you. There was a murder attempt on my moms earlier today and whoever it was knew she was gonna be at the hair salon."

She couldn't believe what she was hearing. It hurt her heart. Ms. Gibbs was cool and she always looked out for Fae when she was growing up. She always let her stay the night knowing what her and Rashawn was doing when she went to sleep. When Kat came into the picture she still treated her good.

"How bad is it?"

He put his head down. "They ain't sure if she'll make it, and if she does she won't be the same. They beat her with metal bats, which triggered a stroke. The doctors are saying that her brain is fucked up. She in surgery now."

"I don't know what to say."

"There's nothing you can say, but there is something you can do. Find out who did this shit to my mother, and bring 'em to me. I got a feeling whoever did this to her is either responsible for my brother's death, or knows who is."

She watched him walk back to the surgical waiting room. She sat on the chair trying to get her mind together. She knew only one person could be responsible for Ms.Gibbs' attack, but she couldn't turn Nyse over to Eric, if she did she knew that Nyse would tell him about the role she played in his brother's death.

CHAPTER 7

Secrets

"Kev, can you make a bottle for me? Make sure you shake it up real good."

Nyse sat in the rocking chair with the baby cradled in her arms. Lil Kevin had been home for a week, and they were finally getting used to his schedule. At first she thought she was going to lose her mind. He had his night and days mixed up. He would stay up all night and sleep most of the day away. That was a complete turn off for her, because it cut into her time with Corey. It didn't help that her and Kevin were on the outs. He had been acting funny towards her since Fae's visit last week.

They went upstairs to talk in private leaving Nyse behind. She didn't care. They did that quite often. Nyse was in a good mood and nothing or nobody was gonna break it. She had gotten word that everything went as planned and she couldn't be happier. About an hour later Fae left out the house without even saying bye. Kevin came down moments later with a solemn look on his face. He didn't say two words to her for the rest of the night. Nyse soon realized what Fae's pop up visit was about.

Kevin came into the nursery with a bottle in his hand. "Thanks, babe." She placed the bottle in his mouth and began to feed him.

Kevin sat on the stool and watched her in her motherly role. His feelings for her were beginning to dwindle. He wanted badly to be there for her and Lil Kevin, but the dumb shit she was doing was making it hard. He knew how to handle the Nelson situation but he didn't know how he could fix the Ms. Gibbs situation. He didn't want to believe Fae when she told him that Nyse may be involved but after he found the court papers in her drawer, he knew Nyse had everything to do with it.

He was the first to admit that he was no saint. Nyse on the other hand was just reckless. She just reacted without thinking and that was dangerous. He wondered why she hadn't come to him when she received the papers. He had *more* than enough money to get a high profile attorney so their son wouldn't be taken. But she didn't. She took matters into her own hands and now she could be looking at an attempted murder charge, or worse, death.

He slowly rose from the stool and went over to the changing table to get a burp cloth. Placing it on her shoulder he bent over and kissed the side of her cheek. She gave him a half smile and continued feeding the baby. Before walking out the room he stopped at the door.

"You know you can trust me right? You and my son mean everything to me, and I will always be there for you, as long as you keep it *real* with me." He said those words with sincerity. He hoped that she would just come out and tell him the truth.

"I love you too, babe." She said without any emotion. She didn't even turn to his direction.

• •

"*Hello you have just reached the voice mail of Officer Corey Hamilton, I cannot come to the phone at this time...*"

Nyse banged the phone down on the receiver. *Where the fuck is he?* She hadn't seen him in a week and it had started to get to her. She sat on the side of her bed with her hands over her head. She had to get out of the house because she was going to go nuts. Kevin had been stuck up her ass all day, on being sentimental. She was not feeling him *at all.* She snickered as she thought about how he expressed his *feelings.*

He thought I was really gonna fall for the punk smooth shit.
"I'll be there for you as long as you keep it real with me," She said in a teasing voice. *Fuck, that!* She thought. She didn't trust him as far as she could throw him and that wasn't far at all. She knew he was just using her, first to get at Spinx, then Rashawn and now her brother. She had come to that conclusion a while ago.

She smoothed her hair out and sat back on the bed. That's when she noticed something sticking out her drawer. She opened it up, and saw the envelope containing the court papers was out of place. She pulled it out and looked inside and they were gone. *That mother fucker!* She ran down the steps.

"Brock! Brock, where you at?!"

Kevin was sitting in the den watching the movie, *'Bout It'*, while drinking Seagram's Gin and Juice. He heard her call his name but decided to ignore her. He knew it was about to be some drama because she was calling him *Brock*. She came storming into the den and stood directly in front of the 52inch screen television.

"You goin' through my shit now? Huh? What happened to that shit you was poppin' earlier?" She said waving the envelope with one hand and the other on her hip.

Kevin took the cap off the bottle of gin and took three huge gulps. He had to get right, because he knew shit was about to get hectic.

"I wouldn't have to go through *your* shit, if you wasn't tryin' to be so fuckin' deceitful." He said calmly.

"Nigga, I ain't gotta tell you every mother fuckin' thang! You ain't got no rings on my fuckin' fingers and you ain't my fuckin Daddy!"

Kevin shook his head trying to keep his poise but he was about to explode. He jumped up off the couch and ran up to her. She jumped back trying to escape but the TV was blocking her.

"Bitch, that's your fucking problem! If you had proper parenting maybe you wouldn't be so fucked up! Maybe I would put a ring on your fuckin' finger if you wasn't around here doin' reckless-petty-shit! You think that shit you doin' is cool? That's your son's grandma you got layin' up in the hospital. She ain't do shit to you! Those court papers ain't mean shit! They had to prove you was unfit, they just couldn't take him."

The spit from his mouth was landing on her face. What really ticked her off was the comment he made about her parents not being around. She had heard enough. She pushed him with all the strength she had. She grabbed her keys from off the kitchen table and ran out the door. Kevin followed behind her hot on her heels.

"Where the fuck you think you goin'? Your son upstairs! You can't leave him!"

Nyse opened the door to her truck jumped in and locked them behind her. She cracked her window just enough for him to hear what she had to say. "That's not my problem! Go tell his dad! Oh yeah...I forgot your *sister* killed him!" She put the key in the ignition and peeled off.

● ●

Nyse drove around the city for an hour. It was late night and she had nowhere to go. She rode down Market Street near 30th and it was packed. She saw some fine ass dudes on Ninja bikes, surrounded by a bunch of tack head broads at the Shell gas station, which was a local hang out on that side of town. The thought of going over there to mingle crossed her mind, but she quickly decided against it. She heard how these chicks got down on the north side, and she didn't need any jealous bitches trying to jump her because she took their shine.

She eventually found herself on Claymont street and noticed *Leroy's* bar was open. She pulled into a run down parking lot across the street and went inside. She wasn't dressed in her usual *go out* attire, and didn't have her fake ID with her. She wore a pair of cut off Daisy Dukes, a fitted Atlanta Braves Jersey and white and red Nike Air Max. By the looks of the place she doubted if they would card her anyway. She went inside and noticed a bunch of old heads sitting at the bar. All eyes were on her as she strutted through the place. She sat at a table over in the corner. She scanned the room hoping she could find some young baller or at least a man who wasn't as old as her father to buy her a drink. She didn't find anyone who fit her criteria that is until she looked to her left.

The man looked to be in his mid 20's, mocha complexion, close cut with deep waves and side burns that formed a neatly trimmed goatee. He wore gaucho style dark denim jeans, with a blue and black Girbaund t-shirt and a fresh pair of "Butters", (timberland boots). Nyse admired him from afar. He wasn't typically what she went for, but there was something about him. He had a serious look on his face, not cracking a smile, nor was he looking at anyone. It was almost as if he was in his own little world.

"Excuse me, Miss, the gentleman at the bar wants to know what you want to drink."

A disgruntled dark skin older woman who looked to be in her late 40's was standing in front of her holding a pen and pad. She wore her hair in ocean waves, and had on a bloody red shade of lipstick. Nyse turned her nose up in disgust. The woman pointed to a toothless old man, sitting at the bar. Nyse's stomach turned immediately.

"Tell him I'm cool, I'm waiting for my *man* to get here." she lied.

The woman sneered. "Your *man*? She looked over at Mr. Man then at Nyse, and then walked away.

Nyse was about to curse her out but she didn't want to get put out. So she sat back in her seat fixed her eyes back on Mr. Man. She was just about to enjoy her view, until she was yet again interrupted. This time a woman who looked familiar to her sat at the table with her. Nyse turned up her nose. *Who the fuck told her she could sit here?* The woman smiled at her and pulled a compact out of her purse and began looking herself over. She ran her hands through her silky black thick hair that was cut into a Chinese bob. She had a dark bronze complexion, big round eyes, with long luxurious fake eyelashes. She was definitely on some Hollywood shit. She put the compact back in her purse and gave Nyse a big grin.

"How's the baby doing?" she said enthusiastically.

"Who are you and how do you know my baby?" Nyse said sarcastically. The woman continued to smile.

"You don't remember me? I was there when he was born. I was your nurse doing the c-section. I'm nurse Hicks, don't you remember?"

She thought about it for a minute. Then it came to her. She did remember her and that's why she looked so familiar. Nyse apologized.

"Oooh, I'm sorry, Nurse Hicks. I remember now, it's been a minute. He's doing well. He's home now with his...um...dad. He thought I needed a break, so I'm just hanging out." Nyse began to smile nervously. She knew the woman knew her real age and she ain't have no business being up in a bar.

"Girl, it's ok, and call me Lynn." She pulled out a twenty-dollar bill. "Gina...Bring me two long islands over here!" Nyse studied Lynn. She didn't look like the type to be up in a bar like this. She looked as if she was a suburban type chick. You know the kind that sat home and drank wine and entertained guest in their big homes. Not drinking Long Island Ice Tea's in some *mom and pop* bar in the city. Gina brought them the drinks and straws. Nyse began to sip on hers and felt her chest burn. Lynn gulped hers down like a fish.

"So, what's up with you and B.I.?" she asked grinning.

Nyse swallowed the contents in her mouth. "Who? B what?"

Lynn nodded her head towards Mr. Man. "B.I., the way you were staring him down I thought y'all had a little something going on. You mean to tell me you don't know who B.I. is?"

Nyse shook her head in confusion. "No, darling. I have never heard of him." She took a sip of her drink like she wasn't impressed.

"Well, let me put it to you this way. He's not to be fucked with. He's a straight lunatic. Nobody fucks with him, including his own family, so watch yourself."

Nyse looked back over at B.I. He didn't look all that danger-ous. She wasn't worried about that anyway. In her mind she wasn't to be fucked with either.

"Where his girl at? I know he got to have a woman unless he gay." Nyse fished.

Lynn giggled and sat her drink down. "Oh baby, he's definite-ly not gay. I heard he had a fierce dick game." She said knowingly.

Lynn filled her in on all the details concerning B.I. Nyse won-dered how she knew so much about him.

"Did you use to deal with him or something? You know an awful lot about him."

Lynn rolled her eyes. "Honey, I am from 22nd and Washington, the heart of the city and I work for Christiana Care. I know a little bit about everybody!" She laughed.

Nyse laughed with her. Her and Lynn had a few more drinks and continued to chitchat. About 2 hours later she was feeling it. She noticed B.I. was still sitting in his corner drinking a Corona. She leaned over and whispered to Lynn. "Girl, watch me bag this nigga." she slurred.

She tried to stand up but stumbled slightly. She caught her bal-ance and put on her sexy walk. Lynn watched in the background silently cheering Nyse on. She pulled the chair out that was on the side of him, slowly sat down and crossed her legs; Giving him a view of her thick firm thighs. B.I. glanced at her and took a swig of his beer. Nyse tried to focus in on his face. Her vision was blurry after down-ing four Long Island's. She did notice that he really was cute. He reminded her of the rapper Nas without the chipped tooth. She smiled seductively. "Hey, I noticed you been sitting here by yourself an awful long time, so I took it upon myself to come join you."

He took another sip of his beer, ignoring her presence. *Playing hard to get huh?* She thought. Nyse was up for the challenge. She was grooving' and needed some nice hard dick up in her.

"So you don't talk? That's cool, because I'm not really into talking either. I'm more into *action*." She said with a twinkle in her eye.

B.I. took the last bit of beer to the head, and placed the bottle back on the table along with a few twenties. He stood up and began walking to the door. Nyse felt her face heat up in embarrassment. *No this bastard didn't just play my face*! That had never happened to her and she felt like shit. She looked over at Lynn for an explanation. Lynn shrugged her shoulders as if to say she didn't know what was up. Just as she was about to talk cash shit to him. She heard him say.

"Yo, young, girl, you comin' or what?

Nyse jumped out of her seat so fast it almost fell over. Deep inside she knew she probably looked desperate and played herself. She didn't care as long as she got what she wanted and that was his attention. B.I. was standing at the door holding the handle. A big smile spread across her face. She hurried to the door but before leaving out she mouthed to Lynn, "I'll get up with you tomorrow." Lynn gave her a thumbs up and she was out.

CHAPTER 8

About His Business

Nyse sat in the passenger side of B.I.'s royal blue 1996 Mazda Millennia. It was tight, fully loaded with mirror tint with blue and black leather interior. He had a hot sound system with a six-disc CD changer. He was blasting a New York mixed tape, *Juice 26,* to be exact. A track with Janet Jackson's, *Anytime,* being rapped over by a Jamaican guy played. *"I know pretty girl her name was Daisy..."* was the only words she understood.

B.I. bopped his head to the beat. He reached over in his glove compartment and pulled out a sandwich bag filled with what appeared to be weed. He cracked his white owl, emptied its contents and filled it with the weed. He then pulled a yellow little baggie halfway filled with a white powder and sprinkled it over the weed. Nyse watched as he rolled and sparked it. Not quite registering what was going on, she accepted the laced blunt he passed her. She took a few deep pulls and felt the effect almost immediately. She couldn't explain the feeling. She wasn't tired like she normally would be when she smoked weed, she felt alive, yet mellow. She was just right. Unknowingly she had just experienced her first "Woolie" weed laced with cocaine.

B.I. started the car and drove off. They got on I-95 North headed toward Chester PA. No words were shared between them; they just enjoyed the music and blazed. Fifteen minutes later they were taking the Ave of the States exit. B.I. turned the music down and dimmed his lights. They crept down what looked to be a side street. Normally

Nyse wouldn't fuck around in Chester, especially at night. That place was dangerous and niggas were known to end up dead fucking around up there.

B.I. pulled over to the side and cut off the car. Nyse attempted to say something but she couldn't move her lips. Her whole body felt numb. He pulled something from under his seat and slid out the car. Nyse noticed two guys who appeared to be ballers standing on the corner. B.I. quietly crept up on them. When he got close enough he pulled a gun from the side of his waist. *Boom. Boom. Boom.* Nyse shook at the sound of the desert eagle letting loose. Her high was immediately ruined by the horrific event that just took place. She nervously fiddled with the door as she watched B.I. rummage through his victim's pockets and boots taking money, jewelry and anything of value. Emotions of both fear and excitement jumbled in her mind. She didn't know if she should hop out the car and get out of dodge or run over and help him rob them.

He casually walked back to the car with his new possessions. He took one look at Nyse who looked as white as a ghost. "What's wrong wit' you young, girl? I thought you said you liked action?" He snickered as he climbed into the driver's seat.

Slightly inching away from him without saying a word, Nyse didn't know how to respond. She wanted to ask him was he fucking crazy. But she already knew the answer to that question. She figured the best thing for her to do was sit back and keep her mouth shut. So she wouldn't end up laid out somewhere dead too.

B.I. could sense her fear. He just laughed to himself and slowly drove off. He watched her carefully as they road back to Wilmington. He wanted to make sure she didn't try to jump out and escape like some of the niggas did when he was handling his business. He could tell Nyse was afraid but she tried hard not to show it and he liked that about her. She wasn't the type of chick he usually dealt with. He liked them chocolate and thick. He wanted a straight up ride or die hood chick that wasn't afraid to bust her guns. To him Nyse looked like one of them Hollywood bitches. The type his people would fall for. Deep inside he knew there was more to her but he knew bitches like her were drama.

He took a leftover roach from his ashtray and sparked it. He inhaled and passed it Nyse. She paused for a moment. He nodded his head edging her on to take it. She took it from him and hit it, then smiled. *She is pretty* he thought. Maybe he could keep her around for a minute.

• •

They pulled up in front of a row home on Concord Avenue twenty minutes later. B.I. jumped out the car and Nyse followed him. Once inside the screened porch, he pulled a key from under the fake green grass rug. He opened the door and the house was pitch black. Nyse couldn't see a thing. She felt him grab her hand and lead her up the steps. They walked down a narrow hallway to another set of steps. Once they reached the top he unlocked the door and they went in. He flicked the lights on which blinded her for a minute after being in darkness. He threw his keys on his dresser and walked to another room, which she discovered was the bathroom.

Nyse looked around checking out her surroundings. From what she could see, he was a neat freak. Everything was in place. All his boots and sneaks were lined up against the wall. Clothes neatly hung and the nigga even had black satin sheets on his bed. She already knew what time it was. So she stripped naked making sure she folded her clothes neatly and sat them on a wooden chair that was by the window. Her head began to feel heavy so she lied back on the bed.

Moments later B.I. came out the bathroom butt ass naked. He looked at Nyse lying on the bed. He had to admit she definitely had it going on. Her body seemed to glow while she layed across the black sheets. He admired her plump ass and couldn't wait to get in between her thick yellow thighs. He walked over to her grabbed both her legs and flipped her on her stomach, which startled Nyse who was half asleep. He hovered over her back rubbing his manhood on the back of her thighs.

"Get on your knees" he ordered. When she was in doggy style position he entered her roughly and began to drill deep into her.

Nyse moaned deeply as he handled her with force. She had never had it like that and she loved every bit of it. He placed his hands around the back of her neck and pushed her face deep into the bed. Nyse began to squirm wildly trying to catch her breath. The more she squirmed the harder he would pound.

"I can't...can't breathe." Her voice was muffled. He began to grunt with excitement and pound her faster.

Sounds of his balls slapping up against her ass and the *aquatic swish* of him moving inside her wetness filled the room. B.I. felt himself getting ready to let loose. He pulled out of her as he rose to his feet and pulled her by the neck off the bed. Her face was beet red and she gasped for air. He pushed her down to her knees and stuck his anaconda down her throat. He knew she was in no shape to perform oral sex. He just loved the feeling of cumming in a nice warm mouth. Three pumps were all it took before he had Nyse swallowing his babies.

He walked over to his side of the bed and pulled the sheets back. "Young girl, turn that light out before you get in the bed."

He turned over and prepared to go to sleep. Nyse collapsed to the floor, her legs were shaking and to her surprise she was still having orgasms. She had never in her life been treated so roughly during sex but what was more shocking was she actually enjoyed it. She gently touched her private parts and winced. Swollen and sore, she slowly got to her feet and walked wide legged to the light switch and turned it off. She laid down in the bed next to him and smiled. *Lynn was right he definitely knows how to handle his business*, were her last thoughts before she drifted to sleep.

CHAPTER 9

Things Ain't How They Should Be

Kevin paced back and forth trying to console Lil Kevin. He had been crying non-stop for the last half an hour. He didn't know what could be wrong. He was fed, changed and bathed. He made sure he had all of his meds on time.

"For you to be so little you got a big ass mouth!" He joked half-heartedly.

Lil Kevin must not have like his joke much because he took his level of screaming up another notch. He couldn't take it anymore. He laid him down in his bassinet and ran to his room looking in drawers in search of the number for the baby's doctor. There had to be something wrong. *The baby wasn't crying for nothing* he thought. He looked through the same drawer he found the court documents in. *Bingo.* He found the discharge/after care folder, which held all of Lil Kev's information. He pulled out the blue sheet and found the number for Al Duponts Pediatric hotline. He picked up the cordless phone next to the bed and dialed the number. The phone rang for what seemed forever. Finally the phone was picked up.

"I need help my son is a preemie and keep cryin'. I think-" He stopped dead in his sentence and immediately become vexed.

"*You have reached the Al DuPont Pediatric hotline at this time all nurses are busy on other calls, leave your name, the child's name and birth date along with your number area code included and someone will be back with you as soon as possible. However, if this is an emergency please hang up immediately and dial 9-1-1."*

"What the fuck!" Kevin hung up and threw the phone on the bed. Lil Kev cried as if he was in pain. Kevin began to rock back in forth holding his head in his hands. "Where the fuck is this bitch at? I swear I'ma kill her when I see her!"

He looked at the clock radio and threw it across the room. It was 4pm and he hadn't heard from her since the argument they had the night before. He tried to call her cell phone but she turned it off. When he noticed she wasn't home that morning he sent his boy Roc out to go look for her but he came up empty. He even called her friend Caree, who said she ain't heard from her in weeks and was packing to go away to college. It was like she disappeared into thin air. He punched the pillow repeatedly wishing it were her face.

After letting out his frustrations, he noticed the crying stopped. He hopped off the bed and ran to the nursery. The worst thoughts were floating through his mind. *What if he stopped breathing?* The baby was sent home with a heart monitor. Kevin wasn't sure if he hooked the baby up to it or not. When he got to the door he sighed in relief. Fae was sitting in the rocking chair patting him on his back.

"How'd you get him to stop crying?" he asked walking over to them.

Fae continued to rub his back. "Gas...he has gas. Did you burp him?"

He playfully smacked himself on his forehead. "Aww shit, I forgot about that!" he laughed.

Fae shook her head and smiled. "Niggaz!"

"I see she got you really playing the daddy role and shit. Where she at the mall with her little friends?"

His smile faded. He pulled a chair up next to her. "I don't know where that broad is. We got into it last night and she rolled out. She ain't been back since. I sent Roc out looking for her and nothing. I even called her girl Caree and she said she ain't heard from her in weeks but I already know that's a fucking lie. Them bitches were yap-

46

ping away last Thursday."

Fae looked down and noticed the baby had fallen asleep. He looked just like Rashawn to her. She couldn't help but feel a little guilty. She was the reason he would never know his real father. She secretly wished she was the mother. Things would have been so different. But that was impossible. Someone took all hopes of her ever becoming a mother away, years ago. She kissed him softly on the cheek and laid him down in his bed.

"So...Ms. Nyse is missing in action. Do you know who else she be with besides Caree? You said she's always vanishing somewhere. You sure she ain't got another nigga?"

Kevin laughed at her remark and waved her off.

"Get the fuck outta here! Naw she ain't cheatin'. She don't even get down like that. Nyse is a lot of things but she ain't no smut bitch. Plus if she was cheatin' I would know for a fact. Ain't shit changed in the bedroom. My dick fits her pussy perfectly." He said in arrogance.

Fae covered her mouth to hide her laughter. "Kevin Brockman...you need to cut the shit! I'll give it to you, you are one sexy motherfucka but you no damn well that lil dick of yours ain't doing her NO justice. She was fucking Spinx and Ra and I *know* personally how Ra-Ra got down. It's a wonder you ain't get lost in the pussy!" She played his face.

Kevin was heated. He hated that Fae knew about his issue. When he was younger he used to have bad seizures and the medicine he took stunted his growth in the place he needed most. That's why he wasn't too quick to sleep with Nyse because he wanted to make sure she was really feeling him before they had sex. That way she wouldn't leave him like the others. The only reason his problem didn't get out to others was because Fae would threaten to fuck them up if they said anything about his problem. He got up and walked out the room.

"Fuck you, Fae!" She followed behind him laughing and apologizing.

"My bad baby but seriously what you gonna do about Nyse?

You know Eric is gonna want to know who did this to his mom and sooner or later he's gonna find out, then he'll find out about what we did and that's a problem." She said with seriousness.

Kevin walked in his room and laid back on the bed. "I don't know sis but you can't lead him to Nyse. You gotta blame that shit on somebody else. I know you can fix it…you always do." He said with confidence.

Fae wished she could agree with him. Her heart was filled with doubt. Nyse really fucked up this time and she had no idea how to make her wrongs right.

● ●

The smell of Hot wings and fries was in the air. Nyse rolled over and smoothed her hand across the bed and noticed she was alone. She sat up in the bed and looked around. She noticed her clothes were still neatly folded on the chair. Next to it was a box of food from New York Fried Chicken. She heard the toilet flush and she attempted to turn in that direction. A prong like pain shot through the back of her neck. *Damn that shit still hurts.* Her whole body was in pain. She massaged her neck.

"I'll have Mia bring you an icepack up for that."

Nyse turned around quickly dismissing the pain. Here she was laid up naked and someone else was up there. She noticed her breasts were slightly exposed and pulled the sheet up covering herself.

"Who are you and where's B.I.?"

Mop-Mop put her hand on her non-existing hips and said with much attitude. "Who am I? Who the fuck is you? This my fuckin' house? Ain't you got no manners?"

Mop-Mop was about 5'4 and thin as a rail. Her wrinkled skin would have made you think she was every bit of 70 years old but the truth was she was only 52. She was a heavy heroin user and B.I. stayed at her house whenever he was in the area. She was like a second mother to him. Nyse was about to curse her out but she opted not

48

to. *What if she was his grandma or something?* She didn't want to make things go sour with her new *man.*

"My bad you just scared me that's all. My name is Nalyse but they call me Nyse." She said cordially.

Mop-Mop looked her up and down. *B done got him a snooty white bitch* she thought. "Nyse, huh? I'm Mophilia but you can call me Mop-Mop. Where you from? The suburbs somewhere? What your mom white or is it your dad?

Nyse laughed at her comment. "I don't know if you would call it the Burbs but I'm from Serenity Hills and I'm full black. No Caucasoid up in me. So where's B.I.?'"

"He out front talking to a few old friends. Where you find him at?" She said with an attitude.

Before she could answer B.I. walked through the door displaying his bare chest. Nyse felt herself get wet all over again. He reminded her of a picture of Tupac when he was laying naked with a bunch gold jewelry covering his manhood. The defined muscles in his arms and chest mesmerized her. She also noticed he wasn't as tall. He had to be about 5'8 at the most. His jeans sagged slightly showing the top of his Ralph Lauren boxers. He walked to the opposite side of the bed and handed her the box of chicken. He then turned his attention to Mop-Mop.

"Moppy, you behaving yourself?" He said giving her a peculiar look followed by a sly smile.

Mop grunted and walked out the door. Nyse was eating a center breast like she never ate before. For some reason she was extra hungry. The chicken tasted extra juicy and the skin was light and crispy. She devoured the meal in ten minutes flat. B.I. laid back on the bed smoking a Newport. He listened to *Champion* by Buru Banton on his Pioneer system.

Nyse wiped her mouth, got up and threw the chicken box away. She went over to his side of the bed and laid her naked body on top of him resting her head on his chest. Nodding his head to the boom of the deep base flowing from his woofers, he continued to smoke his cigarette as he placed his arm around and stroked her back. A feeling of security surrounded her. She found it odd because he was a stranger and a dangerous one at that. She ran her hand up and down his chest and nibbled on his nipple. He moaned. He pulled her face up to his and roughly kissed her, biting down on her bottom lip and sucking her tongue. Nyse moaned in pain. He unbuckled and removed his pants while tonguing her down.

"Give him a kiss for me." He said directing her head to his tool.

Nyse was happy to perform the duty. She opened her mouth as wide as she could and relaxed her throat so she could take every inch of his thickness effortlessly. She slowly glided her tongue in circular motions vertically as she worked her jaw muscles. He gripped her hair and motioned her head in a bobbing motion as he grinded his pelvis to her face.

"Damn young girl, that shit feels good." he moaned.

She became more aroused and placed his balls in his her mouth and hummed, while stroking his dick. He pulled her hair in exhilaration. Nyse was doing her thing and he was enjoying every bit of it. She went back to work on the dick and she could feel a throbbing sensation from him. He was about to bust. He picked up his pace ramming her head deep onto his pole. Nyse held her ground and didn't miss a beat she was sucking the hell out of his dick like a champ. He began to squeeze her ass and breathe deeply and then exploded in her mouth. Nyse came as well. That was the first time she ever had an orgasm from dick sucking alone but it wouldn't be her last.

CHAPTER 10

Love Don't Live Here

Nyse finally decided to return home late that night. Her and B.I. had shared and explored each other in ways she never experienced before. When he took her back to her truck, she asked for a number to keep in contact. "I don't have a number. If you need to get at me, just come around Mop's she knows how to contact me." That didn't sit well with her. She was hoping that he wasn't trying to play her after she sucked his dick, licked his ass and some more shit. He had her open...wide open on some freak shit in less than 24 hours.

"Damn, B...I can't get your number after all we just did?" She whined.

Then it hit her. *He doesn't even know my name.* She shook her head disappointed with herself. She didn't know what had gotten in her. *It must be the weed. That was some bomb ass shit.*

B.I. started his car up. "Look young, girl, I gotta run. Go home wash your ass and get some sleep. Stop by Mop's tomorrow evening and we can chill."

Nyse rolled her eyes as she got out the car. "My *name* is not young girl. It's Nalyse." She said with an attitude slamming the door.

B.I. pulled off. He knew that was all an act because she didn't get her way. He pulled out a blunt he had rolled earlier. *Nalyse...nice name.* He thought.

• •

Kevin sat in the dark smoking a black and mild and drinking Crazy Horse mixed with Seagram's Gin. His plans were for him and Nyse to have a candlelight dinner so they could peacefully discuss their problem. He went as far as having one of his customers that was a chef come over and cook. He even had a sitter for the baby. He sat at the table for hours trying to contain himself praying that she would come home to make things right. He eventually let the thought go and sent everyone home. He grabbed his drink and drank until he couldn't see straight.

He let his thoughts go back to all the warnings he received about Nyse. Fae's warnings being at the top of the list. He began to think she was right. Maybe she was seeing someone else. He remembered how Kat would say she didn't care about no one but herself. In the middle of his thoughts he heard keys rattling in the door. His heart began to pound in anticipation. Kevin quickly hid behind the door.

Nyse quietly opened the door and shut it trying not to make a sound. She locked the door and headed towards the steps. Before she could even lift her foot to attempt to go up, she felt herself being snatched and thrown through the air. She crash-landed into the mahogany and glass end table hitting her jaw on the edge. Her mouth began to immediately fill with blood. Slightly dazed she attempted to rise to her feet by using the table as leverage.

"Where the fuck you been at, Bitch...huh?" Kevin roared. Before she could answer he pulled her up by her hair and slapped her around a few more times.

Nyse staggered before she finally dropped to the floor. She held the side of her face not only in pain but also in shock. She couldn't believe what was taking place. Kevin, the one who claimed he loved her beyond measure was slapping her around like she was some Ho in the streets. Flashbacks of the day Rashawn had abused her resurfaced. She wanted to get up and kill his ass but she didn't have the strength or means to do so. Her only option was to bawl up in a fetal position until he was finished unleashing all of his frustrations.

Kevin stood over top of her ready to deliver another blow. Something stopped him. It was almost as if another person had stepped in his body. He watched her rocking on the floor whimpering. A sense of guilt and shame over took him. He looked at his reflection in the mirror he didn't see himself. He was his father. He stepped back away from the mirror. He held the side of his head and began to shake it vigorously. Kevin was so angry with himself. Tears began to well up in his eyes. He felt that he had to show her a lesson before she got totally out of control. Shit, it worked for his mother. His dad whooped up on her weekly to keep her straight. She was the best mother and wife she could be. Dinner was always cooked, the house stayed clean and she never uttered a word back to his father. She was trained. When he was 13 years old he asked his dad why did he beat on his mother when she did everything she was supposed to do. He told him, "You know how I beat your ass before we go out in public. So you know not to show your ass when we there? It's the same thing with your mother. I call it insurance."

Kevin didn't understand it at the time. But as he grew older and saw how chicks acted up. He knew his father's logic was right. For some reason he just didn't think he would have to do that with Nyse. But he knows that his father is in his grave giving him a handclap for a job well done.

•••

Fae sat at the bar finishing up her third Apple Martini. It was 11:00 in the morning and she was toasted. The meeting she had with Eric had just ended and she was not happy at all with the outcome. He had given her a time frame of 4 days to find out who was behind the brutal beating of his mother. She was beginning to feel like the walls were closing in on her and she had no escape. Anxiety had taken residence in her being and she hadn't felt that way since the night her mother died. Fae sighed deeply and covered her face with both hands. She closed her eyes and the scenes from the horrific night flashed through her mind clear as if she was right there all over again.

"Fee stood in front of her daughter screaming in rage. "Why Fae?! How could you do this to me?!" Fae stood in the bathroom trembling with chunks of brain matter and blood all over her hand and ripped clothing. A lead pipe, which had just fallen from her Fae's hands rested at her bare bloody feet. The body of her mother's lover Sheronda was slumped over with what was left of her battered head in the toilet bowl. Fae cried out and reached for her mother.

"She hurt me mommy. She's been hurting me for years." Fee slapped her only child in the face with all her might. "Stop lying! Just Stop it. You were jealous of us! Nothing good has happened since you were born. I lost my family because of you and now…now you just took away the only person I had left!" She screamed.

Fae felt like her soul had been just ripped from her body. The abuse she suffered at the hands of Sheronda was nothing compare to the hurt she felt from the words that had just came out of her mother's mouth.

"Mommy please, she hurt me. I'm your daughter. I wanted to tell you but she threatened to take you away from me. I just couldn't take it anymore! What are we going to do?" She pleaded.

Fee ignored her and began pulling her friends body from the floor. The right side of her skull was clobbered into pieces. The sight of it drove Fee into hysteria. A demonic howl echoed throughout the house as she sprang to her feet to avenge her fallen lover's death.

Bzzz-Bzzzz…The vibrations from Fae's cell phone startled her bringing her back to her reality. She unclipped the phone from her hip and checked the number. It was Kevin. *Now what?* She thought before she answered the phone.

"What's up?" her voice was weak and slurred.

"Yo, I need you to go over to the house and check on Nyse."

"It's gonna have to wait. I got one of those headaches again. I need to go home and sleep it off." She said rubbing her temples.

"No, you don't understand. This shit right here is serious. I need to make sure she ok."

That got her attention. "What do you mean by that? Where you at? What you do Kev?" she said slightly annoyed.

"Look I can't talk about this over the phone. Just get over there."

The phone went dead in her ear. Fae ran out to her car and peeled off. She braced herself for what she was about to encounter. Knowing her brother and his temper when provoked, he had definitely done a number on Nyse.

CHAPTER 11

Old Habits Never Die

The doorbell rang for the sixth time, followed by a loud banging.

"Who is it!?" Nyse said weakly.

She was still lying on the floor in the same position from the night before. The banging continued. She slowly rose from the floor holding her side that was still in pain from the punishment she endured by her so called "love". She checked her face out in the mirror and noticed the bruises and small cut on the bottom of her chin. *Damn is that all?* She thought he did more damage the way he was wailing on her. She took her hair out the ponytail and brushed it so they would not be visible. The banging and dinging of the bell became more persistent.

"I said I'm coming shit! She yelled annoyed.

She opened the door and Ms. Shepherd's daughter Gee-Gee was standing before her with a baby bag and Lil Kev tucked in her arms. Attitude was all over her coco brown face.

"That's real fucked up how you did my moms. Y'all knew she had to go to church this morning! It's bad enough y'all pay her some bullshit $25 dollars to watch this crying ass baby." She was real ghetto with it. She practically threw the baby at Nyse and dropped the baby bag off of her shoulder. "Next time find somebody else to watch that fuckin' brat." She said as she marched down the steps.

Nyse shook her head in disbelief and picked up the baby bag.

Usually she would have cursed the young girl out but she didn't have time for more drama.

She was about to shut the door when she noticed Fae's car pull up. Today she was driving her black on black Mustang 5.0. It was pretty as shit. She didn't know what type of rims they were but nobody else had them and they were hot. She left the door open and carried the sleeping baby to his room. She gave him a kiss on the forehead and laid him down. She turned to walk out the room but Fae was blocking her way. She sighed and boldly pushed past her. Fae grabbed her roughly and pulled her back facing her. She brushed the hair out of Nyse's face and studied her battle scars.

"Humph, this ain't shit." She said downplaying the seriousness of the abuse.

Nyse immediately became offended. She snatched her arm out of her hand. "It *ain't* shit? What the fuck is that supposed to mean?" Fae smiled with satisfaction. She loved getting under her skin.

"Just like I said, that ain't shit. He's done worse to bitches that didn't do half the shit you do. He definitely has a soft spot for your ass. He's losing his touch. You lucky he didn't put me on assignment. Your stank ass wouldn't be standing here...at...all. So count your blessings, lil' girl. I hope whoever he is was worth getting your ass beat over." She said with a smirk and walked back down the steps.

Nyse took every word Fae said to heart. She didn't know Kevin had a history of being a woman beater. She also knew if he did it once he would do it again. But she knew deep in her heart that he would never sick Fae on her. She walked over to the window and watched her go to her car. Fae looked to the window and winked at her before pulling off. *Bitch.* Nyse had to do something about her situation. She was feeling B.I. to the fullest. Corey was cool too but he was married and a cop. He would only be good for a matter of time. B.I., on the other hand was everything she needed and more. She realized in her mind he was definitely worth the ass kicking.

• •

Two hours later she pulled up in front of Mop-Mop's house. She would have been there sooner but Kevin came back home full of sympathy. He had over a dozen long stem roses and a diamond and ruby 2-karat tennis bracelet. He vowed to never touch her again and he couldn't stand losing her after all that they've been through. Nevertheless, she gave him the cold shoulder packed up her son and headed out the door. He didn't say a word just sat there looking pitiful. In her mind he was pathetic and sick, just like Rashawn and sooner than later he was going to end up like him. Nyse backed into the parking spot with ease. She went into the back of the car and began to undo Lil Kev's car seat. She felt someone tap her shoulder and she was startled. She turned around quickly and noticed Mop-Mop standing behind her.

"Oh my God, where'd you come from? I didn't even see you." She said in a shaky voice holding her chest. Mop looked her up in down carefully examining her.

"Why you look so damn dark in the face? You were a helluva lot lighter the last time I saw ya." She said in an earsplitting voice. Nyse studied Mop's demeanor and came to the conclusion that she was high. She stood with a lean and spoke as if she was hard of hearing. Nyse felt a little uneasy. She didn't want to put her business out there.

"It's make-up. you know foundation…I…um started to break out, and I wanted to cover up the bumps." Mop gave her a look like she didn't believe her. She took a gulp of her Steel Reserve beer eyeing Nyse the entire time. She looked into the car and noticed the baby.

"What ya got there, a baby? Who baby is dat? I hope you ain't tryin' to say it's B's, he ain't been back long enough to get nobody knocked." She said in his defense.

Nyse laughed. "Mop-Mop, you are a damn mess, ain't nobody tryin' to put no baby on B, his dad's name is Kevin." She said pulling him out of the car.

Mop-Mop took a hard look at the baby. There was something

familiar about him. She looked at Nyse suspiciously. "You said his dad's name is Kevin? You sure about that? Cuz this chile looks real familiar he favors..." She went into a deep nod and staggered almost tripping over her own feet. She started talking to herself and walked off.

"Don't mind her. She high right now." A thick young brown skin girl about the same age as Nyse walked down the front steps. She was a cute girl in ghetto fabulous type way. She was no Nyse but she carried herself well. She ran her hands through her 16-inch wet and wavy weave. "My name is Mia. Mop is my mom. So you B's new piece?" She said with a hint of jealousy. She gently took Lil Kev from Nyse. "He's cute...girl. He looks like somebody I know. What's his daddy's name?"

"Nyse ignored her comment. She was tired of her already. "Is B.I. here?" Nyse asked.

Mia laughed. "No he ain't here. He left early this morning and who knows when he'll be back. He does this all the time. Shit, the last time he was gone for years."

Nyse's heart skipped a beat. "Years?" She couldn't imagine him leaving. They didn't even get a chance to get started.

Mia carried the baby inside the house and Nyse followed. "I don't think he's leaving anytime soon. He set up shop again so he'll be around for a minute."

She sighed in relief. That would give her plenty of time to work her magic. It would only be a matter of time before he would be hers.

● ●

Fae pulled up in front of Jael's hair shop. She had a feeling that Jae may know more about Ms. Gibbs' assault than he told the police. She walked into the shop and noticed a new chick at the receptionist desk. She had to be about 16 or so. She was listening to power 99FM and reading a copy of The Source magazine. She was so into her own little world she hadn't noticed Fae come in. She stood in front of the young girl for a few minutes, until she grew bored. She snatched the magazine from her. The girl sucked her teeth. She was about to get smart until she noticed who stood before her.

"Oh...um..hello, Ms. Fatal...I mean Ms. Fae how...how can I help you?" She stuttered with her head down as if she was talking to the floor.

Fae smiled sweetly at the young girl. She was glad to see that she recognized her status. "Where's Jae at I need to talk to him?"

The young girl got up from her seat. "Follow me she in the back."

They both went to the back of the shop where Jael was sitting in his normal chair wearing a silk scarf, tight designer jeans with a fitted shirt and Chinese slippers, talking shit and gossiping. Everyone fell silent when Fae walked through the door. Jael stood up and extended his hands to her.

"Look at you baby, you look fabulous as always. I love the Chinese bob you got going on it really brings your face out. But I got another cut that will fit you perfectly." He said as he guided her to his chair.

"Not today sweetie, but you can curl me up. I might go out tonight." She said. Jae wrapped the black cape round Fae and turned on his stove curlers.

"So, what's up with the new chick out front? Where's Caree?" She asked.

"Girl, she went off to college. She wasn't supposed to leave until next week but after all that mess went down with Ra's mom. she decided to leave early. I guess getting knocked the hell out wasn't in the job description. She never came back afterwards." He said as he parted her hair.

One of his stylist that was there when it all went down added in. "Shit I would have left too if a Nigga hit me the way he hit her. Her shit was swole but at least she ain't get beat down like Ms. Gibbs. I have nightmare's about that shit every night." She said with sadness.

Jael waived her off. "Bitch, you ain't havin' no damn nightmare's. Shit that jacked up a weave is a nightmare!" He said jokingly. Everybody busted out laughing including Fae.

"Ha...Ha...Hell real funny, Jael. You talk cash shit but I ain't see your ass get up and help her when them niggas was beaten' her ass. Your punk ass was over in the corner hidin' and shit, like an ole' bitch." She laughed. Everyone got quiet. Everyone knew that Jael was far from a punk. He had a reputation back in the day before he came out.

"First of all, sweetie, those where not men...those were bitches, two fat bitches with bats...*steel* bats. You think I would take a chance of harming this flawless beautiful face? Hmph, you know you trippin', nobody is worth my demise." He said grooming himself in the mirror. The audience chimed in with their comments. Most of them agreed with him. While others thought someone should have done something.

"No, Babe they were men I know what a woman looks like." The stylist said as she smoothed her hands over her curvaceous body. Jael smirked and sat the comb down.

"Baby doll, I know what men look like in case you forgot I was one and I specializes in mens baby." He said sucking his teeth and rolling his eyes. He played her face. There was nothing else she could say. "Now like I was saying, those were cunts who put a beat down on that old woman. I just don't know what she could have done so bad to deserve it. I heard she's damn near dead!" He shook his head as he curled Fae's hair.

Fae sat back and took everything in. She had definitely gotten the information she was looking for. Unfortunately the news made her assumptions about Nyse's involvement to be correct. From the description Jael just gave, the two chicks were no other than Muff and Buff. They were off limits. Their older brother Switch was a major player in the game. And although Fae feared no one, she didn't want any beef with his army. There was only one expendable option and she was on her way to North Carolina.

CHAPTER 12

Do What I Gotta

Nyse sat on the floor in front of the 32-inch television eating a bowl of Oodles of Noodles while Mia played with Lil Kevin. It was 7pm and there was still no sign of B.I. Mia turned out not be as bad as Nyse thought. After a few hours of chit chatting, she found her to be much like herself. A chick who knew what she wanted and would do whatever to get it. They shared a few of those special blunts that B.I. had given her the night they met. After a few of them Nyse was on cloud nine and really needed the company of her new man. She was horny as hell. Kevin called her phone several times. She answered because she didn't feel like going through the motions when she got home.

"What's up, babe?" she asked flatly.

"I just wanted to know what time you was coming home? It's getting late and I know the baby's tired."

"We'll be there later. I'm chillin' with my girl Mia right now and the baby's fine." She said trying to hide her annoyance.

Kevin sat in silence for a few seconds. "A'ight. I guess I'll see y'all when you get here. I love you." He said in disappointment.

"Yeah, you too." She hung up quickly.

"Who was dat?" Mia asked.

"Damn you all nosey!" Nyse joked.

"It must have been your man?" she said with a grin. Nyse ignored her comment.

She took her bowl into the kitchen. On her way back out she noticed the time. It was getting late and she was thinking it may have been a good idea to take the baby back home. But at the same time she really needed some good sex and she knew she wouldn't be getting that if she went home. She sighed deeply. She really wanted to spend time with B.I but time was running short. Then it came to her. She hadn't talked to Corey in a minute and his sex game was good too. She went out on the porch and dialed his number on her cell phone. He picked up on the first ring.

"Hey, Babe? Where you been? He said with concern.

"I have been around. I just been a little busy. I want to see you. Are you busy?

"Naw...not at all where you at?"

A seductive smile spread across her face. "Meet me at the Sheraton on Delaware Ave in about twenty minutes." He agreed and they said their goodbyes.

Nyse walked back into the house plopped down on the couch next to Mia. "You want to make $50 real quick?" she asked.

"How long you gonna be tramp?" She said playfully.

Nyse took the pillow and swatted her. "Bitch, how you know what I'm about to do!" Mia squinted her eyes and turned up her lips.

"Girl, I'ma pro and I know when a bitch is up to no good. Go do your thing. You better be back by midnight cuz I gotta date!"

Nyse gave her a hug. "You are cool as shit. I really wanted to hang with B.I but my ass needs to get wet. I can't wait around for him. Imma leave my truck here and catch the bus to where I gotta go." Nyse grabbed her purse and keys off the table and was on her way.

• •

Fae sat in her car parked across the street from the greyhound station. After her informational session at Jael's, she decided to reach out to an old friend. She hadn't spoke with Switch in months. The last conversation they had was about a job he had set her up on. He told her he was shocked to hear from her. He told her he heard she had lost her edge after Rashawn's death. It was rumored that Fae was getting out of the business. She reassured him that wasn't the case.

She told him she had another very important job to do and just didn't have time to deal with anyone else's problems until this one was solved. That left him a little puzzled because if she wasn't putting in work why did she call him? She explained that she had a problem and his twin sisters had information that could help solve it. She told him about the attack on Ms. Gibbs and of course he already knew about it. He also knew his sisters, Caree and Nyse were the culprits behind it. He told her that Caree was leaving for school that evening. He was even generous enough to give her the information concerning her departure. In return he didn't want his sisters part mentioned at all. Fae thought that was fair so she agreed.

Her thoughts were interrupted by the sound of the bus's engine. She watched Caree as she and her family shared goodbye hugs and kisses. She boarded the Carolina Trailway Bus with tears in her eyes. The bus slowly began to pull off and her mother embraced her father. They both wore faces of sadness but at the same time beamed with pride as they watched their only child head off to school. Fae pulled a rolled blunt out of her glove compartment, lit it and turned her CD changer to disc 4. She turned it up full blast so she could slip into her zone. She sang along with Tupac. *"Come with me, hail Mary...Run quick see, what do we have here now, Do you wanna ride or die...La dadada...la...la.*

She pulled up slowly next to Caree's parents and rolled down her window. She gave them a sinister smile and blew her smoke out at them. They both looked at each other oddly. She rolled the window back up and pulled off following the bus that carried their daughter. Fae got a kick out of the fact that they had just unofficially met their daughter's murderer and would never know it.

●●

"Whew...Damn! What you missed me that much?" Corey panted heavily as he lie sprawled out across the hotel bed. He just finished round three with Nyse, who was sitting in a straddled position on the side of the bed in anticipation of round four. Nyse rolled her long curly locks of hair around her finger in a seductive manner.

"You know I missed you, baby. Didn't I just prove it to you?" she said in a pouty voice.

"Damn right!"

Nyse smiled and crawled over to him. She could see that he was worn out but she was still horny. Corey did put it down on her but he was no match for B.I and that's what she needed. It was like drinking Kool-Aid on a hot day, knowing damn well water was the only thing that would quench your thirst. But her water was not available so she was determined to fuck Corey until her thirst was satisfied. She grabbed his dead dick, which felt like mush in her hands and attempted to revive it with a little dick to mouth action. She placed it into her mouth and went to work. Corey's eyes rolled in the back of his head while she tried to pleasure him. Pain was what he felt. It was unbearable his shit was sore from all the intense fucking and he couldn't take it anymore. He gently removed her from his manhood.

Nyse had a confused look on her face. She swallowed the saliva that had built up in her mouth. She watched Corey get up from the bed and limp to the bathroom. Anger and disappointment began to build up.

"Baby, what's wrong? What I wasn't sucking it right?" she said with an attitude.

She heard the shower water running. She smiled seductively. *Oh he wants a lil shower action...that's what's up.* She thought. She pranced over to the bathroom and opened the door. She watched as he lathered soap over his muscular body. Her pussy began to pulsate and moisten. She pulled the curtain back and joined him. She planted small kisses along his back and let her hands explore his body. She grabbed his dick again and he slapped her hand away. She stood looking dumbfounded for a brief moment before storming out of the shower. Corey knew that she was upset so he got out to explain himself.

He followed her into the bedroom. He watched her as she gathered her things together. His dick started to rise again at the sight of her wet naked body hurrying around the room. Her body was so firm and curvy. The water looked as if they were beads of crystals glistening on her cream skin.

"Nyse, look baby, I'm sorry. I'm just tired. I had a long day at work and I have to be back there again by 6am. It's already 11:30 and I still have to go home. You know my wife will expect me to give her some too."

Nyse shot him a look of death. "Your wife? Did you just say you can't fuck me because you need to save energy for your wife?" she asked walking towards him slowly.

Corey knew he fucked up. "No, I didn't mean it like that. I didn't mean-"

She cut him off. "Oh, Nigga, you meant everything you just said. Fuck you and your raggedy-ass-not-able-to-carry-a-kid, wife. I don't know why you keep fucking that bitch anyway. It ain't like she gonna *ever* be able to give you a fucking baby. I thought you wanted a baby, Corey. I'm the only one who can do that for you. Not that barren piece of shit wife of yours." She spat.

Her words cut deeply. Corey didn't know how to react. He had never witnessed this behavior from her. He knew she could act bratty and selfish but this was too much. He felt some type of way about the way she was speaking about his wife. True she couldn't have a child for him but he still had love for her regardless. Nyse continued to rant and rave and he grew impatient with her before he knew it he had grabbed her up. He began to shake her like a ragdoll.

"Bitch, don't you ever disrespect my wife like that again!" he said and flung her across the bed.

Nyse landed on her side. She was still in pain from the abuse she received the night before. She knew she had gone overboard by talking recklessly about his wife. But she didn't care. Corey was like everybody else. He didn't love her genuinely. she was something to

66

fulfill what his wife couldn't. She whipped up a few tears and sat up on the bed. Corey was coming towards her.

"Stop, I'm sorry! Please don't hit me again!" she screamed.

Corey stopped in his tracks. He looked at her closely and for the first time that night he noticed the bruises on the side of her body and her face. His heart began to beat fast.

"Baby, I...I didn't mean to...baby who did this to you?" He said as he examined her. He knew damn well he didn't do it not by the little shove he gave her. But he did notice they were fresh bruises.

Nyse flinched at the touch of his hand. "I can't...I can't talk about it." She cried. She jumped up from the bed and started to dress. "I gotta go. I don't want to get in trouble."

Corey was baffled. "What do you mean by get in trouble? Who did this to you? It's ok. You can tell me I can protect you." He said sincerely.

Nyse tried to hide her laughter. He was falling for it. She buttoned her pants and sat next to him.

"You have to promise me that you'll never breathe this information to anyone no matter what happens between us." He agreed. "Kevin...my son's father...he beats me but you have to promise me you won't do anything. He threatened to take my son and he'll have me killed." She said frantically.

Corey sat her on his lap and hugged her tightly. "Baby, he can't harm you or take your baby if he's in jail." He said softly trying to reassure her. She looked him in the eyes and whispered. "Maybe he can't but...She will."

"Who is she, baby?" he asked.

"*She* is who killed my sister, Rashawn and Braxton."

CHAPTER 13

Ms. Bunny

"Who ordered the California Burger with Fries?" shouted the chinky-eyed light skin chick behind the counter. It was 12:30am on a weekday and New York Fried Chicken was jumping as always. This chicken joint was known for getting a late night meal to satisfy your hunger and it was also the place to pick up a young freak joint. Young girls scantly dressed were posted up along the walls in hopes of snagging themselves their next meal ticket and they weren't talking about food.

"That's me babe," he told the woman. "Hold up." Kevin told the woman.

He was huddled in deep conversation with his boys discussing the stick-ups that were occurring. Kevin sat on the ledge of the storefront window in deep thought as he listened to one of his young boys rant on about the latest caper that went down right before his infantile eyes. He was very animated capturing everyone's attention as he spoke.

"I'm telling you I ain't never in my life seen no shit like that. That muthafucka just walked up on dude with the gage, a fuckin' gage at close range and shot that nigga in the dome in broad daylight. So you know what that shit looked like! Bitches and kids was out there, cars were driving by and he ain't have on a mask! He ain't have on anything to cover up his identity. He ain't give a fuck. Yo, then check this, he went into the niggas pockets and socks and took all his loot and went into the store and bought a fuckin' Mystic Fruit Punch!"

Roc shook his head slowly and turned to Kevin. "You know who he's talking about right?"

Kevin swallowed hard and nodded. He knew exactly whom he was referring to. No one else had enough balls to do some shit like that out in the open. He knew he was a real livewire and he didn't want any parts of him. The dude he laid down was actually one of his runners. He knew his crew would expect him to retaliate, but they were young and they didn't know who the unmasked gunman really was and what his capabilities were. He and Roc were the only ones who were old enough to remember how he used to terrorize Wilmington years back, when they were young boys. Everyone feared him but deep down inside wanted to be just like him.

The young boy was hyped. "So Brock, who the fuck is this cat and what we gonna do about him?" He was ready to go to war.

The other youngins looked to Kevin for answers. He took a deep breath and slowly rose up from his seat. He brushed passed the young boy and the rest of the customers in the crowded restaurant, making his way towards the counter to retrieve his food. He left them behind pondering on his actions. It was not the right time to address the issue. He needed time to think things over rationally. He wasn't no punk, but he wasn't stupid either. He never knew anyone who went to battle against that guy and lived to tell about it. He damn sure wasn't about to be another one of his victims by making hasty idiotic decisions especially not over some young nigga that got caught slippin'.

"How much I owe you, sweetie?"

He didn't wait for her to answer. He pulled a wad of cash out of the front pocket of his black Roca wear Jeans. The girl behind the counter eyes twinkled as she watched him peel through six one hundred dollars bills and at least ten fifties before he finally peeled her off a twenty.

She handed him the food and sashayed over to the cash register to make his change. She made sure she put an extra strut in her walk so her ass would jiggle just right to catch his attention. Kevin was shocked when he saw her from the waist down. Waist up, she was built like a regular chick but her hips and ass were ridiculous. He felt his manhood grow when she bent over to pick up the few coins she purposely dropped. He noticed through her canary yellow spandex tights that she wore no panties. Her ass was one of the biggest asses he had seen in his life. She definitely could have been a centerfold for Black Tail magazine. He couldn't keep his eyes off of her.

"Here's your change honey, come again." She said sweetly drawing out the word come. He didn't respond he was in deep thought thinking of what he would do with that fat ass of hers. She began to giggle. "Snap out of it sweetie."

Kevin came out of his trance. He was caught and tried to laugh it off. "Oh, my bad. I just got a lot on my mind. You can keep the change, sweetheart." He laughed nervously.

She put the bills in her bra, exposing her breasts just enough for him to catch a glimpse of her 34 C's.

"Thanks, sweetie. You know I get off in about five minutes, it would be nice if you could give me a ride home."

She caught him off guard. He was about to try and kick game but she beat him to it. She had a sense of aggressiveness to her and that reminded him of Nyse. That's when guilt started to set in. He looked at his watch and it was after 1am. He figured she was most likely home with the baby and waiting for him. He knew that if he took that chick home, he was gonna smash. Then he thought about it. Nyse was acting up and he wasn't sure if she was over the fight they had the other day. He figured if she wasn't he wouldn't be getting no pussy and he needed to relieve stress especially after what his young boys just told him.

"That won't be a problem, sweetheart. I'll be over there chillin' with my people's, come holler at me when you're ready." He said, as he looked her voluptuous body over one more time.

He stepped away with swag as he went back to his seat. His boy Roc wore a huge grin on his face.

"Alright player! I see you, but umm what you think Nyse

70

gonna say about you knockin' off Ms. Bunny." He said playfully punching him in the arm.

Kevin tossed a few fries in his mouth. "Ms. Bunny, who the fuck is that?" he said chewing with his mouth open. Roc and the young boys started laughing.

"You don't know? The light skin broad with the chinky eyes and big ass that you was bustin' it up with just now. That's Ms. Bunny. That bitch like 32 years old. Her daughter is like 16 and that bitch is bad too. She just ain't got as much ass as her mom."

"Yo, she ain't no fuckin' 32. She gotta be about 26 at the most." He said in doubt.

The young boy backed Roc up. "Naw nigga, she is really that old and a freak. Remember that chick Meekie from out The Hills she goes all out like her but real classy with it. She ain't on drugs, or no shit like that but she is about that paper. That's one pussy I'm scared of. Niggas be falling in love with that bitch after just one shot of ass. She got niggas damn near killing each other over her pussy. Ain't no pussy worth dying for." Roc added.

Kevin took two big bites of his burger and handed it over to one of the youngins to throw out. He opened the bottle and took a gulp of his raspberry ice tea before responding.

"Y'all niggas is dumb. Y'all got me mistaken for some of them other lame niggas. I don't care how good her snatch is, I got the baddest bitch in D-ware by my side. That's the only bitch that I'll go to war over and she laying up in my bed right now waiting for her daddy to lay pipe to her ass." He said trying to convince himself.

A few of them snickered, but didn't say anything. They knew Nyse was on some other shit. He was right. She was a *bad bitch,* rotten to the core and everyone knew it. She had been spotted several times flirting with other niggas and Roc could have sworn he saw her going into a hotel earlier on Delaware Ave. It didn't help that she went missing the night before. It pissed him off that his boy got serious with her. He was supposed to just fuck with her to get info on Spinx, but he ended up falling in love. Roc was cool with it at first but lost respect for her after he found out she was carrying Ra's baby knowing he was with her sister. Kevin making her wifey and raising a child that wasn't his really got under Roc's skin. Even though he didn't admit it he knew some how she played a part in the murders that took place a few months back.

Ms. Bunny interrupted their conversation. "Sweetie, you ready to take me home?" she said with a smile as the words ran smoothly from her plump lips.

Everyone got quiet and directed their attention towards Kevin. He stood there in a daze, mesmerized by her soft sensual voice and bodacious body. His manhood began to awaken and his heart raced.

"Baby…are you ready to take me home?" she said again. Kevin came out of his stupor state. He stood up quickly and began to stutter.

"Oh…umm yeah…yeah let's go." He reached for her hand and walked out the door.

When he opened the door he heard his boys clowning him and cracking jokes. They all watched from the window as he opened the door to his black Range Rover helping her and her ass into the truck. Once she was inside he closed the door and gave his boys a wink.

Roc shouted. "Don't get lost in all that ass!" They all laughed and Kevin gave them the finger and drove off.

• •

Nyse opened the door holding Lil' Kevin tightly. She figured if she had the baby in her hands that saves her from getting beat down again. She cautiously shut the door and locked it trying her hardest not to make a sound. It was now 2 o'clock in the morning and she had told Kevin she would be home two hours ago. The living room was pitch black, and she felt along the wall until she found the light switch. To her surprise Kevin was not in his usual spot on the couch downing a bottle of Seagram's. *Maybe he's already passed out.* She thought. *That would be great.*

72

She hoped that he was so tore up that he wouldn't remember that she didn't make it home in time. She tiptoed up the steps and laid the baby in his crib. She began to strip down as she walked down the hallway towards the bedroom. She wanted to be in her proper attire, ass naked. If he saw her fully dressed he would know something was definitely up.

The door to the bedroom was slightly ajar. She peaked in and noticed the bed was untouched. Fear began to set in. She looked around nervously. *Where the fuck is this nigga? Was he watching me?* She opened the closet door quickly and it was empty. She scanned the room again, before she climbed into the bed. She took a deep breath and prayed that he wasn't gonna jump out of nowhere and start whooping her ass. She looked at the clock again. It read 2:20am. She called his cell phone and it went straight to voice mail. She shrugged her shoulders and rested her head on the pillow. *Maybe he's out with his boys,* was her last thought before she drifted off to sleep.

CHAPTER 14

Whipped

These bitches on here are acting a damn fool. The Jerry Springer show was playing on the television. Nyse was sitting on the floor in her living room feeding the baby. It had been two days and Kevin still hadn't returned home. At first she felt some type of way, because he didn't have the decency to call and let her know what was up. He had the nerve to have his boy Roc call her to inform her of his whereabouts.

He had much attitude when he called. "Yo, Brock had to step out for a minute to go handle some business. He'll get at you when he do" and then he banged on her.

She turned up her nose in disgust. *Uneducated bastard.* She knew he didn't really care for her, he showed it every time he was around by dropping slick comments and always talking about all the females they used to be with before her. She didn't feed into him because she truly didn't give a fuck. Kevin could fuck whomever he wanted as long as he ain't bring the shit around her. She didn't plan to be with him much longer anyway. It wouldn't be long before his ass would be locked up. She made sure of that.

Corey had been calling and checking on her around the clock after she spilled the beans the other night. He immediately turned into super cop when he heard the breaking news. No one on the force had been able to find any leads on the case. He had just heard an ear full that would secure him a Lieutenant position for sure with the state police department. Nyse saw how his eyes lit up with excitement. She had to hurry up and bring him down a notch. She made him promise not to do anything with the information she disclosed. The time just wasn't right. Of course it took some convincing, but she was a master of manipulation and by the end of their time spent, he gave her his word. She promised him that he would have his time to shine. Shit, she still had a few loose ends to tie up and once they were secure the shit was gonna hit the fan and she would be with her new man, B.I.

The thought of him made her cream in her pants. He called her early this morning and ordered her to be at Mop's this afternoon. She couldn't wait to hop on his dick and smoke some of that killer chronic. She took the tip of the baby spoon and filled it with applesauce. Lil' Kevin grimaced and began to whine as she wiggled the spoon in his mouth.

"Nigga, shut that shit up!" she barked.

She forced the spoon in his mouth and he let out a loud wail. He was working her nerves. For the last few days she had been stuck with him. At least with Kevin there, he would have him the majority of the time. Normally the baby would be real chill. But for some reason he was on some crybaby shit and she wasn't feeling it in the least bit. She looked at the diamond studded Tiffany's watch that Rashawn had brought back from one of his New York trips and looked at the time. She sighed loudly. The more the baby cried, the more she noticed how much he looked liked Rashawn. It made her sick to her stomach. It was only 12:30pm. The baby's cries became louder. She firmly sat him in the car seat and turned up the volume on the television. He let out a blood-curdling cry.

"Shut the fuck up!" she yelled.

She picked up the phone dialed Ms. Shepherd's number and went over to the dining room. She answered on the first ring.

"*Praise the Lord, Mamie Speaking.*" She sang.

"Ms. Shepherd, I know it's not three yet, but I can't take this!" she said trying to conjure up tears.

"Child, what's wrong and why is that baby screaming like

that." Nyse sensed the panic in her voice and laid it on thick.

"I...I don't know he's been crying all night and Kevin hasn't been home in days. I just can't take it!" She burst out in uncontrollable tears.

Ms. Shepherd sat quietly for a few moments listening to all the commotion on the other end.

"Baby, where's Kevin? What do you mean he hasn't been home in days?" she questioned.

It wasn't like Kevin to up and leave. She knew him since he was a little boy, and she knew how much he loved that baby. She looked at him as if he where her own child and that baby was her grandchild. She really didn't care for Nyse; it was something about her that she couldn't put her finger on. She didn't mind helping her out, because she knew that Nyse had no family left. It was no secret that her mother had disowned her after her sister's death. In her mind the girl had been through too much and was not emotionally fit to care for him properly. But at the same time she felt almost like she was being taken advantage of. She still hadn't run all of her errands, but she didn't have the heart to turn away that baby.

"Baby, get his things together. I'll keep him for a few days, make sure you pack all of his meds and the stroller."

A crooked smile formed across her face, she continued her distress role." Thanks! Thank you so much, Ms. Shepherd. You don't know how much this means to me." She quickly hung up the phone and scooped up the baby.

She cleaned him off and put on his navy blue and green Ralph Lauren sleeper. She emptied out his top drawer of clothes and threw them in her signature Coach diaper bag. She gathered all of his things together in less than ten minutes. She grabbed her car keys off the table and ran out the door.

• •

"Oh my God, girl! What are you trying to do to me?

76

He said clenching his teeth as he received the best head he had in his life. He grabbed a fist full of her silky black hair and pulled harder, which only added more fuel to her fire. Kevin had quickly learned that Bunny was a straight up super freak. She had two tongue rings and her clit was pierced. She fucked him every which way she could for the last couple of days. The shit was so good that he paid her double to stay home from her job at the chicken joint. Not only was she fucking him into a coma on a regular, she could cook her ass off. He had home cooked meals three times a day served to him on a platter, making him feel like the king he thought he was. After each meal she would bless him with mind-boggling head for dessert. Home was the last thing on his mind. Shit why would he go back to what was turning into hell, when he was in heaven?

"Baby, I'mma 'bout to cum." He moaned.

Bunny deep throated him with ease twirling her tongue vigorously around his pint size dick. His body began to shutter as he released his thick load into her wet mouth. She stayed attached to his dick like a baby to a pacifier sucking him dry. He became light headed and his eyes rolled to the back of his head. *Damn Roc was right* he thought before he passed out.

• •

"Who the fuck is that?" Nyse said out loud.

She pulled into a parking spot two spots away from her home.

She watched the short stocky brown haired white boy as he banged on her door. Parked in a driveway sat a dark blue Honda wagon with tinted windows, and a knockin' ass system blasting, Streets of New York by Nas.

She eased out her truck and walked slowly towards the house. When she reached the bottom of the steps, she placed her hands on her hips showing much attitude.

"Umm can I help you?" She asked giving him a stank look. The white boy looked her up and down and smiled. He took a swig off the fifth of Paul Mason he had.

"Damn, what's with the attitude you don't even know me? I could be coming to hand you a million dollars and you treating me like shit?" He laughed.

She looked him over and smirked. From the looks of it she could see him pulling in a few dollars. He was dressed in a pair of Girbaund gaucho shorts, and a black and gold signature Girbaund t-shirt, with Tims. She never understood why niggas wore Tims in the summer it made their feet sweat and left a nasty tan stain on their socks.

"I doubt it very much if you have a *million* dollars, so what's up? What do you *really* want?

He pointed over to the wagon. "My people's wanted to check you out." He sat on the wooden railing and continued to tip his bottle.

She hesitated for a moment, but decided to go over to the car. It was broad daylight, and doubted very much if somebody would try to do some shit to her in broad daylight. Besides no one had enough balls to fuck with her anyway, especially since she was fucking with Kevin, the Northside was his territory.

She walked over to the car and tapped on the driver side window. The driver rolled the window down slowly and a cloud of thick grey smoke escaped smacking her dead in the face. Nyse inhaled deeply trying to suck every inch of it, hoping to at least catch a slight buzz. Once the smoke cleared she expected to see her new flame instead, a semi-familiar face greeted her. He wore his hair braided in cornrows, and reminded her of Snoop Doggy Dog. Nyse stepped back from the car. The passenger door quickly opened and out stepped B.I. Her heart dropped.

He was looking mighty good. His hair was freshly cut and his side burns and goat-tee were trimmed making him look like a million bucks. He wore Jean gaucho's with a hot ass Azzure navy and light blue t-shirt. Something was different about him. That's when she noticed the ice blinging from his wrist. He had on a fly ass diamond studied Rolex that blinded her. He walked over to her and kissed her on the cheek. She felt sparks go through her body as he planted his lips on her. She turned beet red, and dropped her head down in embarrassment. She looked a mess she still had on her pajama shorts, and a pink camisole with no bra and slippers. She was usually on point but she was so quick to get rid of the baby that she didn't think about the way she looked, and that was unusual for her.

"You miss me, babe?" He asked.

She nodded her head as if she were shy. *Babe*? *What happened to him addressing her as young girl*? She wondered.

Snoop Dog's twin, turned the car off and stepped out. He was real flashy with his shit. The nigga was jeweled down. He had to be frost bitten with all the ice he had on. He went to the trunk of the car and pulled out two large brown bags. A sick feeling developed in the pit of her stomach. Something was up.

"Let's go inside I need to holla at you for a minute." B.I. said to Nyse. He noticed the look on her face and knew she was feeling some type of way. "It's cool, babe, these are my people's." He reassured her. He pointed to the white boy. "That's my brotha Hause and that nigga over there is my other brotha. We call him Cousin." He said as he led her to her door.

She stood at the door for a moment before opening it. B.I smiled. That was something she had never seen him do. She noticed he had dimples. "Babe, it's hot ass a mutha fucka out here! Open the door."

She knew what she was about to do could be detrimental but she wasn't thinking rationally. She was stuck and he knew it. She opened the door. B.I walked in first she held the doors as his boys followed. Before she shut the door she looked around to make sure no one was watching. She locked the door and even put the chain on, which was something they rarely used. B.I. and his brothas had already made themselves comfortable in the living room. Cousin pulled out a scale and two bricks of coke, which caused Nyse to panic. B.I. rushed over to her before she opened her mouth.

"Babe, show me your room. I got something for you." He said pulling out two fat blunts.

Her eyes widened at the sight of them. She couldn't wait to wrap her lips around them and him. But she wasn't feeling the scene that was going on. If Kevin walked in on the entire situation, shit was definitely going to get ugly.

"B, what if my baby dad come home, he's gonna flip the fuck out and that nigga can get real raw with it."

He snickered. "Yo, Hause, she said her baby daddy get's real *raw* with it and may not appreciate us invading his home." Taking light of her comment.

Both Hause and Cousin busted out laughing. Cousin picked up a package off the table. "No, nigga this is raw." Referring to the white substance. Hause continued. "You cool, baby girl. We like a challenge every now and then."

He pulled out his German Luger and placed it on the table and Cousin pulled out his 380 Beretta. B.I brushed closely against her body and she felt the steel up against her ass. A sense of security overwhelmed her.

He leaned over and whispered in her ear. "Bae, I got you. The only person you should ever fear is me." Then they both disappeared up the steps.

• •

Ring...Ring. Nyse tried to ignore her cell phone. It had been ringing constantly for the last four hours. She would have turned it off but she was wasted. She and B.I, Cousin, and Mia had been a serious session the night before celebrating her birthday, which was today. They had gone through at least 12 blunts and a gallon of thug passion. They had a suite at the Residence Inn on 273. They were going to be there for the whole weekend. She was laying on B.I's chest. He snored lightly as he held her tightly in his arms. They had been hot and heavy since the day he stopped by the house.

80

She had been spending every night with him since. Kevin didn't mind. He stayed away for six days, and when he finally showed back up, he was cold towards her. He packed a few of his things and said he had to run out of town. Before leaving, he left her a few stacks to handle the bills for her and the baby. Her first reaction was to curse his ass out, and make him feel like shit for neglecting them. But she decided against it because she didn't have time. She knew she had to meet Mia, at the Tri-state mall to pick up some coke bags, and a few other things for the boys. Although, she noticed something was different about Kevin but she couldn't quite put her finger on it.

Nyse rolled the hairs on BI's, hest around her fingertips and ran her tongue around his nipples. He was still half sleep when he moaned. He hugged her tightly then gently pushed her head towards his manhood so she could receive her morning protein. She loved pleasing him. She actually came every time she gave him head. It was just something about that man that drove her over the edge. She became another person when she was with him, doing things she would have never thought she would indulge in. But she didn't care. She had a thing for him in a bad way.

● ●

"Kevin, it's been over a week and she hasn't called to check on the baby. She won't answer her phone when I call. I don't know what to do." Cried Ms. Shepherd.

Kevin sat on the Mahogany Italian leather Couch that he just purchased for Bunny. He was heated. He couldn't believe that Nyse had dumped her son on the woman. The more she talked, the more he wanted to go beat the shit out of her. He perished the thought when he realized that he was as wrong as she was. Still, suddenly, he had taken on the responsibility of full-time daddy.

"I'm sorry about this, Ms. Shepherd. I'll be there to pick him up in a few and Ms. Shepherd, thanks for looking out for my son." He said before he hung up.

"Stupid Bitch!" He yelled as he flung the phone across the room, which went crashing against the wall. Bunny came running out the kitchen, wearing nothing but a bright green thong, and slippers with a spatula in her hand.

"Sweetie, what's wrong with you?" She said making her way over to comfort her new moneyman. She sat her over sized ass on his lap and stroked the side of his face. "What's the matter, daddy?" She said stroking his ego.

He moved her off of him and grabbed his air force ones from off the steps and began to put them on. *No this nigga didn't just push me to the side.* She was offended by his rude behavior. She moved to the love seat and watched him as he hurried around the house gathering his things. She had the right mind to cuss his little-dick having ass out and tell him how his broad was over on Concord Ave, fucking with that crazy nigga and getting high on woo blunts. That would definitely break him down but she decided to let it ride. Besides she had plans and she wasn't going to let anything this petty detour them.

See, Bunny knew more about Brock aka Kevin Brockman than she let on. She knew everything there was to know about him, his little toy girlfriend and the so-called son he was raising. She had her eye on him for a minute now and was just waiting for the right opportunity to dig her claws into him. What Brock didn't know was that he wasn't the only fool Bunny had sprung on her pussy.

Young Nelson was also addicted to the voluptuous vixen. He met her right after Ra and his sister were murdered. He was chillin' at the Casbar over Southbridge with his boys celebrating the life of his deceased boss. When Bunny walked in all eyes were on her. She wore a bright orange one-piece halter short set that clung to every curve of her body, with gold sandals. Her hair was flat ironed and hung right beneath her chin, which made her facial features more prominent. She sat down at the bar and ordered her usual drink, a Midori sour and waited to be approached. She knew tonight the ballers were going to be out but she wasn't just looking for anyone, she wanted one in particular. Who happened to be 18-year old Nelson

"Stack" Nyse. Everybody knew that Ra-Ra had made him his successor; which meant the youngin' was about to be highly sought after. However, she was determined to snag him and turn him out before any of the young girls got him and she did just that.

Things were hot and heavy between the two. She remembered one night she was lying in the bed, and he told her everything about his family and how he believed his sister may have had something to do with Ra's death. She listened attentively as he spoke about the business and admitted his insecurities about being able to carry them out. He also told her that Brock was stepping in on his territory and he didn't know if he had enough manpower to stop him from taking over completely. Ever since then she looked at him in a different light. She knew he wasn't going to last long so she turned her attention to the next man who was about to take over.

Brock grabbed his keys from off the table and headed to the door. *Do something. You can't just let him walk out the door*, she thought. She jumped from the love seat and ran up the steps. She grabbed the first thing she saw on her bed, which happened to be a purple and silver DKNY tank dress. She slid into the dress and ran down the steps, when she heard the screen door slam. She opened the front door as Brock started his truck.

"Wait! Baby, wait a minute!" She yelled as she ran almost tripping down the front steps.

Kevin watched with an annoyed look on his face. He put the truck in reverse but stopped when he noticed his passenger door fly open. He put the car back in park and turned his attention to Bunny.

"Yo, what's up with you? I told you I had to go!" He snapped.

Bunny tried to catch her breath before she spoke. "Look Brock, I know I haven't known you all that long but I wanted to let you know I am really feeling you. I know that you have a family but, sweetie you don't deserve what's happening to you. From what I can tell you're a good man and I don't want to lose you. The last few days have been wonderful and I just don't want to let that go. I care about you, and I'm willing to do whatever needs to be done to be with you." She said trying to sound as sincere as possible.

Kevin listened to her every word. He wanted to believe it to be true but he knew her type. She was about that dollar. She had a good shot of ass and made him feel like a king but he couldn't allow himself, no matter how much he wanted to fall for her bullshit. He smirked and shook his head.

"Bitch, save that shit you just like all the rest of those hood rat smuts. You ain't feeling me. You like that cash that I spent on ya ass and that vicious pipe I be laying to you. I ain't like the rest of those niggas you be fuckin' wit. A good shot ain't gonna make me leave my family. You can beat it, bitch cause I got shit I need to handle!" He said in arrogance.

Bunny's face turned beet red. She felt herself ready to explode inside. *Laying vicious pipe! What drug is this mutha fucka taking?* She thought. She had never in her life been that humiliated. She felt tears of anger welling up in her eyes. She was about to lash out on his ass but reminded herself of the bigger picture. She had to play her part so she swallowed her pride and gently spoke as the tears dropped.

"I...I know you don't mean what you said but I understand your frustration. I'm gonna let you handle your situation but I want you to know I meant everything I said. I'll be waiting for you and *our* son to return." She leaned over and kissed him on the cheek before getting out the truck.

He watched her as she walked up the steps. He wanted to feel bad for her but he couldn't. His mind was on his son and that was his main focus. If what she was saying had any truth to it she would be there when he was done.

CHAPTER 15

Sibling Rivalry

"Bitch, where the fuck you think we going?" Laughed Mia pointing at Nyse.

Nyse stood on Mops porch caressing her body. "What, Bitch! It's my birthday; baby and you know I gotta be fly! Shit this is the new me and I'm stepping out tonight baby!"

Nyse was feeling herself. She had a complete make over she dyed her hair honey brown with fire engine red highlights that were spiraled curled up into a Chinese pony tail. She wore a fitted champagne colored Chanel corset style dress with five inch Jimmy Choo pumps to match. Kat's five-karat canary yellow diamond necklace set it off even more. She took it after Kat died to have something to remember her by. She was fierce and she knew it. Today was her twentieth birthday and she was feeling herself. They were on their way to the Safari Lounge on Lancaster Ave.

"Look at you looking like a fake ass high class Charlie Baltimore! Bitch, we ain't going to the country club!"

Nyse ignored her as she strutted pass her. "Bitch, I'mma boss and I have to stay on my "A" game. You'll never catch me lookin' a hot mess." She said in confidence.

Mia followed her to the truck. Once inside Nyse started it up and turned on her latest Selecta Bam Bam mix CD. Lady Saw's Ninja Bike blared through the system. They pulled off and headed towards the Westside. Mia pulled out a Newport cigarette along with a little vile which was filled with a substance that resembled Muslim oil. Mia took the cigarette and dipped it inside the vile.

"What's that?" Nyse asked.

Mia lit the cigarette and took a deep pull. She passed it to Nyse.

"Umm-umm honey, I don't do cigarettes that's shit is unattractive." She said with her nose turned up.

Mia rolled her eyes. "Bitch, please! You smoke more weed than a lil' bit. How you gonna act funny about a laced newt. It ain't no different from smoking Woolie's." She said with a slight attitude.

Nyse ignored her last comment. She really didn't know what a Woolie was she guessed it was just another name for weed.

"What's that shit you dipped it into?" She inquired.

Mia looked at her as if she was crazy. "Are you serious? It's the shit they make wet from. It's not that bad just take a few hits you'll be feeling all the way live. It's the shit."

Nyse thought about it for a minute. It couldn't hurt. Besides it was her birthday. She took the cigarette from her and took two pulls. At first she didn't feel anything but once they reached Lancaster Ave, she felt her head get heavy. She wasn't feeling this type of high at all. She looked into her Jimmy Choo clutch bag and retrieved the blunt B.I had given her earlier. She sparked it and her and Mia shared it before entering the bar. After a few hits, the high began to level itself out. She was on cloud nine and felt as if she was floating when she made her way in.

The bar was packed niggas and bitches were everywhere. Most of them were dressed regular, so Nyse was most definitely the center of attention. It was as if time stopped when she walked in up on the scene. Niggas jaws dropped as well as a few bitches. She and Mia posted up in the corner at the bar. Nyse scanned the room to see if she saw anyone familiar but no one caught her eye. The bartender came over to them and they both ordered a Cosmo. Normally she would have felt apprehensive because she was in enemy territory. But not tonight. She felt invincible. She didn't know if it was the drugs or the fact that her new man was a force to be reckoned with.

The drinks came back and the girls clicked their glasses together as if they were making a toast and took sips from the straws. They were in their own little world having a private party until Nyse felt someone brush against her. She slowly turned around and noticed a guy with a mocha complexion and extremely long dreds standing behind her. Nyse turned her nose up and was about to break him down right quick. She wasn't into foreigners and from the looks of it he was a straight Rasta.

"What's that you're sippin' on?" He asked. His voice was smooth and showed no trace of a West Indian accent.

Mia whispered in her ear. "Bitch, don't act shitty this nigga got paper. He runs with those niggas from 27th and Tatnall. Check out the Presidential Rolie he sporting."

Nyse directed her attention to his wrist and it almost blinded her. Her attitude did a complete 360. *Tatnall huh, that's Kevin's territory.* She thought. That made her even more fascinated and up for the challenge. She flashed him her award-winning smile and batted her eyelashes. She gave a girlish grin and said. "A Cosmo."

The guy sat on a bar stool next to her. He ordered another Cosmo for her and Mia.

"So what brings someone as beautiful as you out tonight? I've never seen you in here before." He asked as he pulled out a knot of money to pay for the drinks. Nyse didn't pay any attention to the money that wasn't her thing. She was more on a power trip. But Mia on the other hand was creaming in her panties.

A smile of satisfaction crept across his face when he saw that she passed the test. He would always throw money on the table to see how the female's reaction would be. That's how he separated the gold digging one-night stands away from the potential wifey status chicks. He knew there was something familiar about her when he saw her walk through the door. Everything about her said high maintenance and sent up a gold digger alert. But she had a sense of class either she had her own loot, or she had a nigga who was big in the game.

K.D. Harris   87

"So what brings you out tonight, young lady?"

"It's my birthday, I'm celebrating, my name is Nyse and you are?"

"They call me Jab, happy birthday. How old did you turn today, Ms. Nyse?" Nyse took a sip of her drink and twirled the straw around her tongue in a seductive manner.

"Old enough." She moaned. She winked at him and placed her hand on his thigh and ran her tongue over her lips. She felt her body heat rise and she felt her womanhood awaken. This was not her normal thing. It had to be the alcohol. She ran her fingers through his locks and whispered in his ear.

"*I already know what you want, so let's not beat around the bush. You probably have been on me for a minute. I know you know my man, Brock and I really don't give a fuck. It's my birthday and that nigga ain't even have the decency to spend it with me.*" She stood up from the stool and circled around him as if she was modeling.

"Would you let all of this go out to the club to be devoured by wolves if I was your girl?" She asked.

Yo what the fuck is wrong with Brock? That nigga is whack. Jab now knew why she was familiar. Brock was his connect and he had seen her in the car with him a few times. But she didn't look as fine as she did tonight. She looked like a straight up video vixen, like she needed to be on the cover of Source, or Don Diva. His mouth watered, as he thought about all the things he wanted to do to her. The ringing of his cell phone interrupted his thoughts. He looked down at the screen and it was his brother's number followed by the code 187.

"Fuck!" He said out loud.

Nyse nodded her head. "That's what I'm talking about." She said completely oblivious to what he was talking about. She thought he was referring to getting their night started in a quieter place.

"Naw babe, I'ma have to take a rain check. I gotta bounce." He gave her a quick kiss on the cheek and placed a wad of cash in her bra. "Happy birthday!" He said before exiting the bar.

Nyse stood with her jaw dropped. Mia turned the other way

trying to hide her laughter. Nyse came up behind her and playfully slapped her in the back of the neck.

"What the fuck was that shit, that nigga just bounced on me? She said in shock.

Mia busted out laughing. "That's what your nasty ass get! You should be happy he bounced what was you gonna tell B.I when we go back to the room? You know he was gonna be able to tell that you was fucking another nigga right before him. He would have kicked your Ho ass to the curb."

Nyse rolled her eyes. She knew Mia was right but she wasn't going to admit it. With the way she was feeling she could have gone a few rounds with that Jab character. The bulge in his pants looked as if he could put it down too. She ordered a Long Island ice tea compliments of Jab. She pulled the money he left out of her bra and counted it. He was very generous and gave her a little over $900. She smiled and knew she would definitely be making a trip to 27th and Tatnall in the near future.

Jump spread out do it, and move your body, jump spread out do it.... rang through the speakers. Nyse took her drink to the head like a champ and jumped from her seat.

"Hey, that's my shit!" She yelled grabbing Mia by the hand so they can hit the dance floor.

They both moved their bodies seductively to the reggae beat, putting on a show for the onlookers. Nyse was at one with the music, gyrating her hips and caressing her herself. Dropping down to the floor she did the latest dance, *"The Cry Baby"*. Mia joined her and the crowd went crazy. The DJ changed up the mood by putting on a little Baltimore Club music. *"If it's your birthday make noise"* blared through the speakers. The girls jumped up and went wild. Nyse was so into it she didn't even know the last person she wanted to see was sitting in front watching her the entire time.

• •

Bunny found it amusing to watch the infamous Nyse in action. *Now I see why that nigga stays stressed out.* She rubbed Stack's back as he stood their glaring. From the looks of it she wouldn't be surprised if he went out there and snapped her neck right in front of everyone.

"Baby it's ok. Let's just go." She whispered in his ear. He shook his head in disgust.

"No fuck that! We ain't going nowhere!" He snapped.

Stack couldn't believe his eyes. It was almost as if he had seen a ghost. He couldn't believe how much Nyse looked like Kat. To him it was almost like she was trying to be her. Her body had filled out. Her hair was no longer radiant black. Now it was the same as Kat's. Her clothes were also like Kat's. What really had him heated was the necklace that Rashawn bought her the night they got engaged. He knew it because he was at the party. His stomach curled at the sight of her. Kat would never act like that. She had too much class. No matter how much Nyse tried she would never measure up to Kat. It was too much for him to take. He went over to the floor and grabbed her by her arm.

"Who the fuck!" she stopped in the middle of her sentence when she saw who had grabbed a hold of her.

"Well...well look what we have here."

"Hey, little brother you came to help your big sister celebrate her birthday? Oh I know it's been a minute but I wanted to tell you I love the way you and your little friends redecorated my apartment." She said sarcastically.

She snatched away from him, went to the bar and ordered another Long Island. She watched her brother out of the corner of her eye. He was still looking dumb in the face. His gear was on point and she had to admit that he was iced out. She did notice he didn't have an entourage like Rashawan kept. He had a few young boys with him that she had never seen with him in the past. She also noticed the chick who looked like she was too old to be with him.

Nyse took a good glance over Bunny's body and noticed how

90

wide her hips were and the ridiculous ass she had in tote. Nyse smirked. "That's what it is." She said out loud.

"That's what...what is? Ain't that your brother over there?" Mia asked confused.

"Her big ass is what? That bitch looks to be every bit of 30. My brother is only 18. Why else would he be with her? It has to be the sex." She said with an attitude. She took another sip of her drink. Her mood was beginning to shift and she didn't like it. It was her birthday and she wasn't about to let her brother spoil it.

Mia looked over at Bunny and laughed. "Who? Bunny? Girl, if your brother is fucking with her it's over. She is a man-eater! If she ever get's a hold of your nigga, its a wrap for whoever she's with. She is a beast at her fuck game. Shit I want to be just like her when I grow up." She said in admiration.

Nyse rolled her eyes. "Whatever."

She looked down at her watch and noticed it was only 11:45 pm. It was still early and she had 15 minutes before her birthday was officially over. She scanned the room to see if there was anyone else she could fuck with just to keep her mind off of Stack. The sad thing was she wasn't going to be able to get off that easy because Stack couldn't keep his eyes off of her. Part of him was happy to see her. But as he thought about it more, he realized the pleasure came from Nyse's uncanny resemblance to Kat.

He kept picturing Kat in the coffin, and then to see Nyse trying to take over her life was a hard pill for him to swallow. He got up from his table, swiftly making his way to her side. He acted out on his emotions. He turned her around on the bar stool and slapped her across the face. Then he snatched the $25,000 necklace from her neck. Mia tried to shield Nyse from the next hit but it didn't work. He caught her again. Only this time he ripped the front of her dress exposing her breasts. Mia wrapped her arms around Nyse to cover her friend up.

"Help, somebody help!" She screamed.

Nyse tried to break free from Mia to get at her brother.

"Fuck you, nigga! I swear to God you gonna die mutha fucka!

You gonna be dead just like your faggot ass boss!" She yelled.

She was hurt, not physically because he hit like a bitch. She was embarrassed and couldn't believe he went on her like that. People started to vacate the premises knowing things were about to get hectic.

"Bitch, fuck you! You ain't gonna kill shit. I got something for you and I hope you tell your gay ass boyfriend. He knows where to find me, bitch! Stop trying to be her! You'll never be her, bitch! It should have been you who took that bullet, you scandalous ass trick!"

Nyse began to laugh wickedly. "Don't worry mother fucker you'll be able to see your precious sister again real soon. I promise you that...I promise!" She picked up a bottle of Moet that was sitting next to her and aimed it at his head but instead of hitting him, the bottle hit Bunny.

Blood ran down the side of her face. She began to scream. "Oh my God! Oh my God!"

At the sight of the blood Stack panicked, pulled out his .38 and busted in his sister's direction. She was already headed out of the door before he noticed he shot the wrong person.

POISON

TWO

A FATAL ATTRACTION

CHAPTER 16

Innocent Bystanders

"*Everything is a go...meet me tomorrow at the Hilton in downtown Raleigh room 217*" Fatal hung up the phone.

She stood in line waiting for her turn to enter Club *Plum Crazy*. This was a hot spot for the college kids on Thursday nights. She had been following Caree and found this to be one of her favorite spots. She and a few of her friends had arrived 45 minutes earlier. Fatal blended in perfectly with the other students. She wore her hair in a rod weave ponytail and a Roc-a-wear jean dress with a pair of Reebok classics. She didn't want to be too over dressed. Her regular attire would have drawn too much attention to her.

This guy who looked liked "Old Dirty Bastard" kept bumping up against her. She knew what his deal was but she wasn't feeding into him. He was straight country with a mouth full of gold teeth. His dress game was whack and he had dragon breath. He bumped up against her again with more force. Fae tried to control herself. She had the right mind to spit the razor out of her mouth and slice his damn throat. Instead she kept her composure and turned towards him slowly.

He slapped hands with his boy, who actually didn't look half bad, like he conquered something. "What up sexy? You from up North?" He said in a southern draw.

Fae shook her head in disgust not only did he look a mess but his game was trash too. She opened her mouth to curse him out but something caught her attention. She noticed Caree hanging on some guy leaving out the club. Fae watched them for a moment then made her way back to the car. She watched them get into a silver Honda Civic. Moments later they pulled off. She waited a few seconds and followed behind them. *This is some bullshit she thought to herself.* She was on a time limit. Eric would be in town tomorrow and shit had to go smoothly in order to get him off of her back. He was losing patience with her. She could tell by the conversations. She knew he really felt some type of way for her leaving town without telling him. Some things were just better left unsaid. She knew if she told him he would be full of questions and she didn't have all the answers.

The car pulled up into the Capital Inn parking lot. Caree and the guy both exited the car and went into the rental office. *Damn.* Fae punched the steering wheel in vexation. She was getting angrier by the minute. *Why the fuck she ain't keep her ass in the car?* That would've made it so much easier to snatch her up. She needed to relieve some stress. She looked in her ashtray and found a roach. She lit it and took a few puffs. She felt her cell phone vibrate next to her. She looked at the number and laughed. It was Nyse. *Kevin must have whooped her ass again.* She pushed the end button to ignore her. She took another long pull and closed her eyes. The vibrating started again. It was Nyse. *Man, what the fuck?* She answered the phone with an attitude.

"Yeah?!"

She heard a bunch of ruckus in the background. Somebody was yelling and screaming, and music blared.

"*Fae! I need you that mother fucker tried to kill me!*" Nyse yelled. It sounded as if she was crying. Fae tried to hold her laughter. She figured Kevin really fucked her up. She wondered what she did to deserve it.

"Where's my brother at?" She asked flatly.

"I don't fucking know! I'm on Concord Ave, I went out for my birthday at the Safari and my brother and some bitch came up in there acting weak. We argued and then he shot at me! I swear to God I want that nigga dead, I don't care how much it cost! I want him gone

94

tonight!" She cried. As she was listening to her story she noticed the couple leaving out the office. They walked over to a room on the second floor. She turned her attention back to the conversation.

"Yo, I'm handling some business. I'll get at you when I get home." She hung up the phone and opened her car door.

She went up the opposite stairs and headed towards the room they entered. She had to think quick on her feet. Her original plans where altered since Caree wanted to smut around. She paused at the door before knocking. She hoped the guy would open it. She listened closely and heard his voice. *That's what I'm talking about.* He cracked the door and peeked out.

"Can I help you? His eyes ran up and down her body admiring what he saw. Fae saw that he was digging her and decided to use it to her advantage.

"Umm, I'm in the room across the hall and I noticed my roommate come in here with you. I needed to give her the dorm key because I don't think I'll be making it home tonight but from the looks of you I doubt it if she'll be making it there either." She giggled seductively. She pushed the door opened and looked around for Caree and didn't see her.

A sly grin spread across his face. "Naw, she'll be back before you know it but once you're done with dude, why don't you come by and pay me a visit?" He said licking his lips. She looked him over and milk was definitely doing his body good. She figured he was a football player.

She sat on the wooden table and gapped her legs open for him to sneak a peak. "Who ever said it was a guy I was with?" Fae teased.

His eyes widened and she could see the print in his pants begin to rise. He pressed up against her and ran his hands up her thighs and kissed her on the neck. "You smell so good." He whispered. The door to the bathroom opened up and Caree appeared wearing nothing but a towel. The first thing she saw was her new friend hugged up with some bitch.

"Oh hell no, nigga!" She blurted before she charged at him. He moved away from Fae quickly and dodged the blow that was coming towards him.

"Baby wait, she came on to me!" He shouted as he tried to protect himself. Caree was so busy wailing on him she didn't realize that the chick he was hugged up with was no other than Fae.

Fae laughed at the show that was going on in front of her. She couldn't believe how the nigga bitched up. *I guess they just don't make niggas like they used too.* They crashed into the nightstand and the lamp blew out causing the room to go dim. The people next door banged on the wall and that's when Fae decided to end it. She didn't need anyone else coming into the picture. "Hey cut that shit out…that's enough!"

Caree turned around to get at her. "Bitch, I don't–" She paused when saw who was standing before her. "Oh shit!" She said backing away from her.

Fae smiled and walked towards her. "What was that you said, Caree? I didn't quite *hear* you." She kept the smile on her face, which freaked Caree out even more.

The guy got up from the floor holding his arm. "You stupid bitch! You broke the fuckin skin! I ain't gonna be able to play right tomorrow!" He examined the humungous bite mark she left on his arm. Fae turned her nose up at his whiny ass.

"Nigga, stop bitchin' and get your punk ass up outta here." He looked at her like she was crazy and put on his tough act.

"Bitch, I ain't going no fuckin' where I paid for this fuckin' room! You get the fuck!" He grabbed Fae by the arm.

Caree held her chest and pleaded with him. "Don't do that!"

But it was too late. Before she could get the last word out Fae had already whipped out her blade and ran it across his throat. Blood began to rapidly leak from the fresh cut. He stumbled around the room in a panic as he tried to hold his neck in an attempt to stop the bleeding.

"Oh God…Please don't kill me!" She begged.

Fae wiped the blood on her pants from the razor and popped it back in her mouth. The taste of his blood lingered. She spit it out and grabbed a handful of Caree's braids. Caree was about to scream.

Fae put her finger up to her lips. "You don't want to do that. You may end up like your little friend."

Caree watched him as he twitched on the floor gagging on his own blood. She cringed in fear to Fae's satisfaction. Although she didn't know it, Fae had no intention of harming her. She was more important to her alive than dead but she wasn't going to let her know that.

"Get your things together and let's go." She ordered. Caree hurried and scooped up her items. Fae walked over to the door but before she opened it she warned her. "I mean it…don't try no slick shit." Caree nodded in agreement.

"I won't, but what about him?" She pointed to the dude who was now lying unconscious on the floor.

Fae shrugged her shoulders "Fuck em" She said as she opened the door.

• •

The look in Stack's eyes when the bottle hit his girl pierced like a dagger to Nyse's heart. What really hurt her is when she noticed him heading towards the bulge in his waist. Never in a million years would she have guessed her own flesh and blood would have tried to take her life over some *trash* bitch.

Soon as she saw his hand reach for is gun she darted towards the door leaving Mia behind. She heard the gun let off and ran up the street for safety. She was afraid to get into her truck not knowing if he would follow her there. She didn't know what else to do but run. She held her top together as best as she could as she ran down Lancaster Avenue. A black Acura legend sped up beside her. Not knowing if it was her brother or one of his boys she began to scream frantically drawing attention to herself. Hoping someone would come to her rescue.

The door opened and Nyse was half way relieved when she

noticed who jumped out the car. It was the guy Jab she had just met.

"Come on get in the car." He said leading her to the back seat.

Nyse didn't think twice. Once inside she noticed he wasn't alone. He had two other dudes in the car. Panic began to set in and she went to open the door but he already pulled off. Here she was half naked with hood niggas she didn't even know.

"Let me out! Just let me out!" She screamed. The guy next to her was staring at her semi bare chest. Tears fell like puddles. "Please don't do nothing to me. It's my birthday!"

The guy next to her busted out laughing. "Yo, this broad is crazy!"

Jab looked back at her in the rear view mirror. "I'm not gonna hurt you. I was on my way back to scoop you up and that's when I noticed you running out the bar. What happened in there and where your girl at?"

"They started shooting and …I ran. I think Mia is still in there. We need to go back and get her." She pleaded.

They circled around the block and noticed the club was now flooded with Wilmington Police and a few ambulances. He parked at the corner of Lancaster and Franklin.

"Wait right here." He ordered. Him and his boys exited his car.

Nyse rolled down the window, halfway trying to hear what people where saying. She picked up her phone and called Fatal. She knew she could work something out with her to have Stack taken care of. She didn't answer on the first ring, so she called again. This time she answered. But too much dismay, Fae didn't seem the bit interested in anything she had to say. That didn't do nothing but add fuel to her fire.

"Fuck that dyke!" She yelled as she kicked the seat.

She was about to call Kevin but that wasn't going to do anything but cause more issues. She thought about B.I but she had no number to reach him. She thought about having him paged at the hotel but it wasn't guaranteed that he would be there. She was stuck.

A half hour later the group returned to the car. This time Jab sat in the back seat next to her. He wore a solemn look on his face. Nyse knew something was up immediately.

"Where's Mia?" She asked frantically. Jab looked down before answering. "Where the fuck is she at!" She cried.

"Yo, what *really* happened in there?" He asked ignoring her question.

Nyse unlocked the door and tried to open it, he slammed it shut. "Let me go if you don't want to tell me, I'll find out my damn self."

"Calm down! Your girl didn't make it. The bullet that was meant for *you* hit her in the head. They she said she died instantly."

CHAPTER 17

The Sweetest Thing

"You ready little man?" Kevin asked Lil' Kev as he buckled him in the seat belt.

The baby blew spit bubbles and cooed at his father. Kevin shut the door and hopped in and started up his truck. He rode to Concord Ave and noticed a bunch of cars parked in front of "The Spot". The Spot was a house owned by a fiend that was well acquainted with his newfound enemy. *I wonder what the fuck is going on there.*

He rode passed the house slowly trying to see if he could catch glimpse of him. Someone did catch his eye. A chick that he could have sworn was Nyse stood on the porch talking to a group of people. The only thing that stopped him from investigating further was the fact that this chick's hair was blond with some red shit up in it. He hadn't seen her in a few days and she didn't even bring her ass home last night. He figured she was pissed because he didn't call her and tell her happy birthday. He was really getting tired of her ass. He sped up in case someone noticed him creeping. He didn't want no shit when he had his son with him.

He turned down the side street that led to Washington Street. He parked in front of New York Fried chicken hoping to find Bunny so he could apologize. He went inside the empty store and went straight to the counter.

"Yo, where Bunny at?" He asked the guy cooking the fries.

"Bunny not here. She quit!" He said with an Arabic accent.

Kevin got back in the car and busted a u-turn in the middle of the street. He turned up 24th and pulled up in front of Bunny's house. He took the baby out the car along with the diaper bag. He knocked on the door and waited for her to answer. He knocked a few more times before it was finally answered. Her daughter came to the door wearing a tight red Dickie shirt with a red tube top. She was absolutely her mother's daughter her body was banging. Kevin couldn't even look at her.

"Your mom here?" He asked looking away.

She opened the door to let him in. "Brock...right?" He nodded his head.

"Oh she upstairs. I think she sleep though she just got home from the hospital a few hours ago. Is that your son?" She asked reaching for him.

"Yeah that's my lil' dude but why was your mom at the hospital?" He asked with concern. Her daughter took the baby from him and headed towards the steps.

"She got hit in the face with a bottle. I don't know all the details. You're gonna have to ask her but she should be lucky she ain't end up like Mop daughter. She got shot square in the head and now she dead."

So that's why all those people where at the house. Damn. He knew Mop had a daughter but he didn't pay her any attention. All the chicks from that area were on some slimy shit and he ain't fuck with them. Still, he ain't wish death upon nobody who didn't deserve it. He followed her up the steps to Bunny's room.

She opened the door for him then disappeared down the hall with the baby. Bunny was lying on top of her turquoise satin sheets wearing nothing but an over sized T-shirt that fit loosely but hugged her hips. He took his boots off and laid in the bed next to her pulling her body close to him by the waist. He ran his fingers through her hair and pulled it back so he could check her face out. It was covered by a large bandage that was over half of her ear and went as far down as her chin. She turned over and opened her eyes.

"So you decided to come back? You may not want me when these bandages come off." She said in a groggy voice. Kevin kissed her softly on the lips.

"Baby, what happened?" He said stroking her face. She sat up in the bed.

"I don't really want to talk about it right now?" She said holding her face. "It's still hurting like hell."

He gave her a hug and kissed her again. "I'm sorry, I feel like I'm some what responsible. If I didn't act like an asshole yesterday this could have been prevented. I brought my son with me today. I wanted you to meet him."

Bunny's face lit up. "Really, where's he at? Bring him here I want to see him."

"Your daughter has him. Let me go get him for you." He hurried down the hall to get him. Bunny clapped her hands together. *I got this bitch now.*

As a woman she knew that it was a no-no for another chick to play stepmom to your kid. Bunny wasn't really for raising another baby but if it meant securing her future she would do whatever she had to. She wanted to tell Kevin everything but she had to plan everything carefully. She wanted Nyse to pay for what she had done to her. She scarred her for life and she wanted her to pay with hers. She wasn't too thrilled with Stacks either. At first she thought he fired the shot in her defense. Then she realized that it was in his own defense when he left her there bleeding. He didn't even call to see if she was okay. It was all-good with her though. Because when she was done she would be the victorious one and Stacks and Nyse would be yesterday's news.

• •

Nyse sat on Mop's porch feeling as if her head was about to explode. She was being interrogated by Mop's family and friends about what happened the night before. She could tell a few of them did not believe her story.

"Why the fuck would you leave my niece when you saw a gun being pulled?" Her aunt pointed her bony black finger in her face.

She had her hair braided in two braids on the side of her head. Her face was ashy and she had three teeth missing in the front. Nyse wanted to curse her crack head ass out but she knew they were in their feelings.

"I don't know it just happened so fast. I thought she was behind me. What would you have done if you were in my situation?" She challenged her.

The woman walked away cursing out loud calling Nyse a bunch a white bitches. One of her brothers tried to calm her down. Nyse buried her face in her hands. *This shit is out of control.* She said under her breath. The house was crowded with Mia's friends who all blamed Nyse for her demise. She wanted to go in their and fuck one chick up in particular who was talking reckless.

"That bitch don't do nothing but cause drama! She the one who had her boyfriend, along with her sister and her sister's fiancé killed a few months ago. She be fucking with that crazy bitch Fatal. It ain't no secret that she was involved. She just ain't get caught. She probably set Mia up too!" The chicken head said.

Nyse wanted to go in there and rip her tongue out of her mouth but she was in no mood to be fighting. Besides she would most likely get jumped on by all those bitches including the crack head aunt.

The only reason why she stayed there was too talk to Mop and B.I. The only two in her book who really mattered. But that didn't seem like it was going to happen. B.I never showed. Instead Cousin and Hause stopped by to drop Money off for Mop to help with the funeral. Cousin acted like his normal self by cracking jokes, and even tried to talk to one of Mia's cousin. She couldn't believe it. She thought he really was feeling Mia. She wasn't even in the grave and he was already trying to get in some new pussy. *Niggas!*

"You alright?" Hause sat next to Nyse in one of the green plastic lawn chairs. He offered her some of the Henny he was sippin' on.

She declined.

"I'm cool. Does B.I even know what happened? I thought he would be here by now. I know he was close to Mia."

"Oh he knows what's up. B.I's a different type of nigga. It's too many people over here. He more private…He'll pop up when you least expect. That's just him but wherever he is, he's cool." Hause explained.

He took the rest of the bottle to the head. Nyse shifted in her seat trying to get comfortable and the plastic chair began to stick to her ass. She needed to get home and change. Mia was bigger at the bottom than Nyse was and she swam in her shorts. The tube top fit perfectly but she still wasn't feeling her attire and she needed a shower.

"Hause, do me a favor, let Mop know that I'mma stop back later to make sure she's alright. I need to go home and get my mind right. You got something for me?" He knew exactly what she was talking about and he handed her two woolie's.

She was about to stand up but she noticed a group of girls that looked to be in their early teens walking up the steps with a baby. The girl holding the baby was dressed like a straight smut but there was something about her that looked familiar. She was brown skin with almond shaped eyes and her skin was flawless. Her body was ridiculous and she made Nyse look like an Aids case. Nyse figured she had to be about 14 or 15 with a baby. *I bet she don't even know who the daddy is. She just looks like the loose type.*

"What's up Lil' mama, who kid you got?" asked Hause.

The young girl answered." Oh this is my moms new friend son, ain't he cute?" She bent over to show him the baby. Being nosey Nyse snuck a peak and had to do a double take. *What the fuck*! She almost shit herself.

"Hold the fuck up! I know that ain't my fuckin' son!" She snatched the baby from the girl and sure enough it was Lil' Kevin. Nyse jumped in the young girls face.

"How the fuck did you get my baby?"

The girl didn't show any fear. She had enough nerve to even laugh. "Miss, his dad said I could bring him outside. If you have a problem you can march your happy ass over to 305 W. 24th street and handle it with him." She looked at one of her friends who were ready to jump on Nyse at a moments notice. "My mom is gonna get a kick out this shit!" She bumped Nyse as she walked in the house.

Nyse was heated. She wanted to beat the shit out of the disrespectful brat. But she had other shit to deal with. She went around the corner in search of her truck. Jab had one of his boy's drop it off hours ago and told her it would be on the side street with the keys in the visor. She saw it parked on the corner. She threw the baby in the seat without strapping him in and rode around the corner to W. 24th.

She pulled in front of the address and sure enough there was Kevin's truck. She popped open the trunk and got out the car. She was in search of her faithful Louisville Slugger but it wasn't there. She did spot a hammer and a gasoline can. She beamed deviously. *I got something for his ass!* She grabbed the hammer and can and went to the back of her car to get an old newspaper. She took the claw side of the hammer and flattened each one of the tires on his truck. She busted out the back window causing his alarm to sound she unlocked the door and dumped as much of the gasoline she could inside of the car. By the time she got finished pouring, the screen door flew open. Kevin had on a pair of boxers with nothing else.

"What the fuck!"

Kevin couldn't believe what he was seeing all four tires were flat to the rim. He grabbed his waist and realized he didn't have his gun. *Damn.* He ran down the steps to get a closer look to see who was vandalizing his property.

Nyse came around from the back of the truck with the newspaper and Hammer in hand. Kevin stopped in his tracks. He couldn't believe it. She was the same chick he saw on the porch.

"Yo, what the fuck is up with you? Are you fucking crazy and what did you do with your hair?"

Nyse leaned against his truck laughing. "No nigga, your ass is crazy. How the fuck you gonna have my baby up at some bitches house? Then have the audacity to have her trifling ass daughter parade him around like y'all some happy little family and shit. I'm not playing that shit. That's my mother fuckin' son, not yours you need to remember that! Now where's the bitch you playing house with so I can let her ass know where the fuck she stands. Lil' Kevin has one mother and that's me! So get your bitch!"

Kevin couldn't believe what was happening. "Why were you on the Ave? Who you know over there?" He said changing the subject. Something wasn't quite adding up and he feared for the worst. *I know this bitch ain't fuckin with that nigga.*

Before she could answer the question Nyse was in for an even bigger shock. The chick that she hit with the bottle appeared at the door wearing nothing but a sheet and a sneaky smile. Nyse was enraged. She ran towards her but Kevin grabbed her and tried to get the hammer out her hand. Nyse stomped on his bare feet with her sandal and bit him on the shoulder and he let her go. Bunny slammed the door shut before Nyse could get to her.

"Fuck you! I swear to God I'mma fucking kill you, bitch!" She screamed at the top of her lungs. She looked at Kevin and spit at him. "Don't you ever come near me and my son again! I fucking hate you!" Kevin wiped the spit from his face.

"Where the fuck you gonna go at? You ain't got no family or friends! All you got is me! Ain't nobody gonna want you! Everybody know your ass is Poison! You're no fucking good! Everything you fuck with turns to shit! You just mad because I found a better mother to take care of my son, you dizzy bitch! You'll never see him again if it's up to me!"

Nyse rolled her eyes and shook her head. She took the lighter from her pocket and lit the newspaper.

"Baby, it's not possible to keep something away from a person when they already got it!" She threw the newspaper into the back of the truck and everything went up in flames.

106

A FATAL ATTRACTION

CHAPTER 18

Birth of Fatal

Fatal sat on the edge of the metal chair eating a banana and flipping through the latest issue of Vogue magazine. A black and white photo of Richard Geer was on one of the pages. He was advertising some type of cologne.

"Whew, if I was into white men, I would give him some. Ain't he sexy?" She squealed as she tried to show her the picture. "Mmm...Oh, I forgot you can't see...my bad" She laughed.

Fae was being sarcastic. She knew Caree couldn't see anything. Both of her eyes were swollen shut from the beating she put down on her.

They had pulled up to the local Krispy Kreme donut spot to pick up breakfast. Caree decided to get slick and act like she had to go to the bathroom. Fae went to the counter to order while she went into the bathroom. When Fae got back to the car she noticed Caree was taking too long. She went into the bathroom to check on her and noticed it was empty.

Fae hurried to the car and pulled of in search of her. She found her five minutes later running towards Shaw University where she went to school. Fae was happy that it was still dark outside. She jumped out the car and zapped her with the stun gun and drug her back to the car. She was going to take her back to the Hilton where she could at least enjoy a little luxury before she finished her off. Instead she took her to an abandoned shack she found on an old dirt road.

The house was old and rickety and smelled of rodents. It would do the trick. She only needed it for a minute anyway. Once inside the house Fae made her strip naked and beat her senseless for being disobedient. When she woke up she tied her hands behind her back. Then she took a noose type rope and found a sturdy beam. She tied one end of the rope to it and slipped the other end around her neck. Fae forced her to stand on a chair. Caree begged and pleaded.

"Fae, please don't do this! I'm so sorry I'll do anything! Please I'll tell you whatever you want to know."

"Who said I wanted *you* to tell me anything? I already know what I need to know. I have you here because I want to make a deal with you. I need for you to play a little game with me. I have a client that I am working for and I haven't quite completed the job. I already know who is really responsible for the act but I just can't get to her right now. So I need you to take responsibility for her actions. In return, I'll give you half of the money he gives me but you have to never return to Delaware again."

"What is it? I'll do it! Whatever it is! I just want to leave with my life."

Fae smiled with satisfaction." Good, I need you to take responsibility for what went down with Ms. Gibbs."

"What! Why? Who cares about what happens to her? She was pure evil."

Fae crossed her legs and sat back in the chair. "I agree, she is a work of art but I ain't got nothing but love for her and so does her son."

Caree's foot almost slipped from the chair. Fae jumped up and held her steady. "Be careful honey. If you slip that's it for you." She joked but was dead serious at the same time.

"Her son? What son? Ra-Ra is dead!"

Fae chuckled. "Sweetheart, she had two boys, Eric and Rashawn. Eric is Ra's older brother. He should be about 30 now if I'm not mistaken."

Caree couldn't believe it. She wished she could see Fatal's

face to see if she was joking or not.

"Nyse never said anything about him. I never heard anything about no brother."

"Why would she tell you anything about him? She didn't know herself. She barely knew Rashawn. I'm not even sure if Kat knew who he really was. Ms. Gibbs and Eric didn't have the best relationship when he was growing up. She said Eric had the devil in him. She often told people he was a bad influence and for them to keep their kids away from him. She was right. He was a bad influence. Shit, how do you think I turned out the way I did?" She snorted.

"How...how did you get to be the way you are?" Caree swallowed deeply hoping she didn't just earn herself an early death.

Fae sat silent for a moment and took a deep breath. "I don't think you could handle the truth about me. Not many people can."

She looked at her watch and noticed she still had hours before Eric would show up. Fae never told anyone what really happened the night her life changed. She figured it wouldn't hurt to tell her. It's not like she would be able to ever tell anyone else anyway. She kicked her shoes off and propped her feet on an old dusty TV.

"My mother's name was Fee I loved her with all my heart. It had been just me and her most of my life until I was about 11 years old. She let her "friend" Sheronda move in. Everything was cool at first. Sheronda treated me as if I was her own child. We went to the Brandywine zoo, the library and she would take me skating every Saturday.

"After about four months of her staying with us things began to change. Sheronda and my mother began being more distant from me. She even moved out of the room she occupied and into my mother's bedroom. I was young I didn't understand what was going on at first but I soon found out. My mother cleaned offices for DuPont and one night she ended up staying a little later because she had to do two buildings. I was in my room playing my Lisa Lisa and Cult Jam tape in my Walkman. Sheronda came in the room and climbed underneath the covers with me. I remember it like yesterday.

"It was winter time and her hands were cold as ice her breath wreaked of Mad Dog 20/20. She began to touch on me in places that weren't supposed to be touched. I froze up because I didn't know what to do. I wanted to tell her to stop but words couldn't escape my lips. After she was done she told me to never tell my mother. She said if I did she would take her away from me and I would never see her again. She knew that my mother was all that I had. Afterwards I felt really weird and wondered why she did those things to another girl. I felt like I wasn't normal anymore. So that's when I started to run with Ra-Ra and his crew and acting like the boys. But there was something in me still that needed a man.

"When I was 12 I was over at Ra's eating dinner and Eric came in. He must have just pulled one of his capers because he was real antsy. I was used to him being on edge but today was different. I looked down at his feet and I noticed blood all over his boots. I tried to act like I didn't see it but he already saw that I noticed. *Fae come mere' let me talk to you for a minute.* He told me.

"I followed him to his room and he shut the door and locked it. He took his boots off and tossed them in a plastic bag. He told me to take his boots to Brandywine and burn them. He gave me everything I needed to carry out the deed. He said, '*Yo, I really need you to do this right, don't be all nervous just keep your composure at all times and no one will ever suspect you of anything.*' He pulled out a wad of cash and handed it to me. When I was on my way out the door he said. '*I know what's going on at your house and when you're finally fed up I can help you make your problems disappear.*'

"I did as I was told and everything went smoothly. After that we became cool and he had me do little jobs for him on the low. I guess you can say I became his protégé. He even taught me how to fuck Ra-Ra the right way. I know it sounds crazy but I was young and I looked up to him and I owed him a lot.

"When I was fifteen I got pregnant. I didn't know if it was Eric's or Ra's. I would have rather it had been Ra's because I loved him and I wanted it to be his so he could leave that bitch Kat alone.

Sheronda was still molesting me on a regular but it seemed when she caught on that I was having sex she became more violent with me and my mom. At this point I was starting to wonder if my mom knew what she was up to because she barely said two words to me.

"I came home late one night, me and Eric had been at this old head's crib that he stayed with over on Northside. He moved out of his mother's house a few months prior because she stabbed him in the neck. She thought he had turned Ra onto hustling. I told him about the pregnancy that night. He didn't have much to say because he wasn't a man of many words. So, I went to my room and noticed everything on my dresser was knocked off. I went to my mom's room to find out what was up and she wasn't there.

"When I came out Sheronda was standing in front of my room with a wire hanger in her hand. I didn't know what was up with her so I walked past her and into the bathroom. When I tried to shut the door she pushed it in. I said, '*I need to pee, could you excuse me please.*' She acted as if she didn't hear what I was saying and stood in the door staring at me with this stupid look on her face. She said, '*You little dirty bitch you done went and got pregnant on me!*' Then she balled up her fist and punched me in the nose. Blood started to gush out. I tried to rush her but she out weighed me. She beat the shit out of me in that bathroom. *'If I can't have no damn babies neither will your trifling ass!'* She screamed at me.

"My body was so weak and all I could do was cry and pray that someone would save me but they didn't. She shoved that coat hanger repeatedly up in me until huge clots ran down my legs. I was in so much pain I wanted to die. I lay in the bathroom all night in a bloody puddle. I wanted to die but I didn't. A week later Sheronda, after my bruises healed up, took me to the hospital. She told them some bullshit story. She told them I confided in her and that I took the coat hanger and aborted my baby. Of course they believed her. They did the examination and gave me the worst news of my life. They said that I had done so much damage that I caused massive scarring and would never be able to have children." Fae paused and tears started to fall.

Caree felt her pain. She wanted to tell Fae she was so sorry but decided to keep quiet.

"I was not the same afterwards. After we left the hospital I went over to where Eric stayed and told him everything. He didn't say anything but I knew he was hurt because I could see his eyes tearing up. He didn't have any children and I know he secretly hoped that the baby would have been his.

"He looked at me with all seriousness and said, '*Are you tired yet?*' I nodded my head yes. Then he went over how I was going to get rid of my problem. Later that night I went home and as usual my mother wasn't there but Sheronda was. She was sitting at the small table in our kitchen eating hot dogs and baked beans. I did my usual routine by going to my room, taking my bath and preparing for bed. After my bath I went back into the bathroom to brush my teeth. Usually, I did all of that when I took my bath and I knew Sheronda would be waiting for me in my room since my mother wasn't due home for another hour.

"Sheronda marched down to the bathroom with an attitude. She busted through the door. '*Hurry the fuck up! We ain't got all day! You know Fee will be home soon.*' She yelled at me. I ignored her and continued to brush my teeth. I had on a pair of tight little panties and a sports bra. I had started to fill out more due to the pregnancy and I knew Sheronda was liking what she saw.

"She rubbed her hand over my ass. She locked the bathroom door. '*We might as well do what we gotta do in here. Take those panties off.*' She ordered. A sick feeling came over me. I turned the water off and put my toothbrush back in the holder. I purposely knocked it over. I bent over to retrieve it. When I stood back up I had a lead pipe that Eric had placed in the bathroom. I took the pipe and wacked her in the face with it. She fell into the door but quickly got back up. Blood was pouring from her face. '*I'mma kill you!*' She screamed.

"She rushed towards me and I caught her again, this time in the back of the head. She fell and her head hit the toilet. For some reason I got excited when I saw the blood coming from her. I closed my eyes and just wailed on her. I felt so liberated. Then I heard the front door open. I panicked! My mother was home early! I looked around the bathroom and it was a bloody mess. I didn't even have a chance to clean it up and get rid of the body. Before I knew it the bathroom door was rattling. *'Open the door I need to pee!'* She yelled. I slowly unlocked the door and she came in. I will never forget the look in her eyes when she saw Sheronda's dead body slumped into the toilet. She blamed me for everything, even said I was jealous.

"I tried to tell her what she had done to me but she didn't believe me. She made me angry when I saw her picking up chunks of her brain trying to piece it back together. That's when I realized how pathetic she was. I pleaded with her to hear me out. Instead she tried to attack me and that's when I snapped.

"She grabbed me by the throat and we both fell into the tub knocking the shower curtain down. That's when she saw that we weren't alone. Eric was there on standby like we planned. He pulled her off of me and handed me his .9 milli. I didn't think twice when I pulled the trigger. I didn't have any remorse when I saw my mother lying dead next to my abuser…her lover. But that wasn't the end of my problem. My mother had someone outside waiting for her. Mrs. Brockman, who was my mother's supervisor, had given my mother a ride home and was waiting outside to take my mom food shopping.

"She sent her son Kevin in to see what was taking her so long. Kevin stood in the hallway in total shock. He had just witnessed everything. *'I promise I won't tell just don't do nothing to me,'* he begged. Eric ordered him to tell his mother that her mom changed her mind and that he was gonna stay and chill with Fae for a while. He did as he was told. Eric included him in our plan and since Kevin was a nerd in school and a great kid the story would be believable.

"When the cops came they believed everything we said that someone came in the house and tied us up and killed my mother and her girlfriend. Come to find out Sheronda had a bad gambling problem so it wasn't a shock what happened to her. I ended up going into to foster care and after a month I ended up staying with Mrs. Brockman. A year later Eric went on a robbing and killing spree and disappeared no one heard from him until now. So that's my story."

She killed her own mother...No wonder she's so fucked up. Caree wasn't sure if she wanted to meet this Eric character. From what she just learned, he was worse than Fae. She figured she better cooperate or she would end up like Fae's mother and girlfriend or worse.

"Ok, I'll go along with it."

Fae nodded her head in satisfaction. "Great"! She untied the noose around her neck and allowed her to sit in the chair and relax, while she schooled her on what to say.

• •

Four hours later Fae received a phone call. It was Eric. She gave him the directions to the house and he said he would be there in five minutes. Fae helped Caree to her feet.

"What...what's going on?" She asked hysterically.

"He's here. I can't just have you chillin' and shit. We have to make this as real as possible. So you have to put this back around your neck."

Caree whined but did as she was told she wanted to get this out the way so she could move on with her life. She took her place on the chair and held as still as possible. For some reason it felt as if Fae made the rope around her neck extra snug. She could barely swallow. A few minutes later she heard the door creak open and a male's voice.

"Fatal, where you at?" He yelled through the shack.

Fae came through an opening from the back of the house. "Hey how was your drive down?" She asked cheerfully.

"I ain't got all day! I need to get back up the way. Some shit went down that I need to handle. So let's get this over with. Where she at?" His tone was stern.

Fae's smile dropped from her face and she led him to Caree.

114

A small smile crept on Eric's face when he saw Caree standing on the chair butt as naked with her hands tied up and a noose around her neck. What he wasn't feeling was the fact he couldn't look her in the eyes since they were swollen shut. He wanted to be able to look her in the eyes when he questioned her. He believed that you can see what people where about from their eye movements.

"I see you're still creative with your shit but what's up with her eyes? You know how I feel about that shit." He scolded her.

Fae put her head down and began to kick the dirt around on the floor like she was a little girl being chastised by her father whom she adored.

"Sorry, Eric, but she tried to run, so I had to teach her a lesson." She said sounding pitiful. Eric shook his head in disappointment. He then turned his attention towards Caree.

"What's your beef with Eliza Gibbs?"

Caree didn't say anything. Eric looked at Fae and gave her the *do something look*. Fae went over to her and inched the chair away causing her to lose balance. She began to stumble.

"I …I didn't like her. She was always mean to me."

Eric twisted his face up in confusion. "Mean? You damn near have a 50-year-old woman beat to death because she's mean? Naw it has to be more to it than that."

Caree began to shake uncontrollably. His voice was full of rage and it scared her.

"Yes, she was real mean and nobody liked her. I didn't mean for...I mean I just wanted to scare her!" She blurted. She began to cry uncontrollably. "I'm so sorry, I didn't want to…I…"

Fae began to panic. *This bitch is loosing it that is not what I told her to say.* Fae had to think fast. She wanted to shut Caree up fast before they both ended up dead. She went over to the chair but Eric beat her to it. He pulled it out from underneath her. Caree's body jerked as she struggled to keep her breath. Eric then put the chair back under her feet and ordered Fae to hold her steady.

Caree coughed and panted trying to catch her breath. Eric was infuriated.

"Now are you ready to tell me the truth? Or do I need to give you a taste of what I do to people who *I* think is mean?"

Urine ran down Caree's legs. She knew that she wasn't going to get out this alive if she didn't tell him something. "I...I did it because she tried ...to keep ... Ra away from me. She was so into that bitch Kat. I just..." She sobbed.

Eric shook his head in disbelief he knew she was lying through her teeth. He had heard enough.

"Fatal, finish this bitch!" He commanded.

"No!!! Wait. I'll tell you the truth—" Fae quickly pulled her chair next to hers stood on it and placed a potato sack drenched in gasoline over her head. Before tying it she whispered in her ear. "I told you to stick to the plan. You just committed suicide." She pulled a lighter from her pocket and ignited the sack.

Caree shrieked in anguish as her head burned. Her body convulsed violently causing her to loose footage and slip from the chair.

Fae and Eric both watched as her body burned to a crisp.

CHAPTER 19

"Here, give Mop this for me." Nyse handed Hause an envelope with a check to help towards the funeral, which was being held today at St. Paul's church on Market St. He took the envelope.

"Are you sure you don't want to go?" He asked as he dusted off his black Stacey Adams shoes.

"Naw, I've had enough of funerals this year. I must say you know how to clean yourself up well, baby." She joked as she admired Hause. He was dressed in all black compliments of Armani, of course. She never was into white boys but Hause was alright.

"Do you think that B.I will be there?" Nyse hadn't seen or heard from him since the morning of her birthday.

Hause said that he was handling some business and would be back soon. She wanted to know where he was at and why he always disappeared so much. She didn't even know his real name. She made up in her mind that she was going to get to know more about him he was such a mystery.

"I couldn't even tell you. I don't think he the funeral type dude though. He ain't even go to…" He stopped in the middle of his sentence. He bit his bottom lip.

He didn't go where?" Nyse asked enthused. *Got em'!* She figured Hause was about to slip up some information on B.I.

"Naw, it ain't nothin'. Look I'll check you later. Cousin gonna stop by too and check on you later." He hurried out the door before something else came out.

Nyse chuckled to herself. *He's hiding something, but what could it be.* She climbed out of bed and went to the bathroom. She looked in the mirror and didn't recognize herself. Her eyes sported bags and dark circles and her pupils looked large and dull. *Bitch you need to get yourself together, you're falling apart.* She looked at the small box of a bathroom and laughed in disgust.

This is what I've resorted too in a week's time. She turned on the water in the sink until it ran steaming hot. She looked at how pale her face looked with the blond hair. She could pass for a white girl with a tan. She took the washrag and wet it with the steamy water and she placed it on her face and she felt her pores opening. It burned like hell but at the same time it was refreshing. She sat on the floor in Indian style and held the rag on her face. She thought about how her life had been spiraling down hill over the last few months.

None of her goals where accomplished. She was so caught up in chasing a nigga she realized that she neglected her number one priority. She should have been focusing on getting revenge on all those who played a part in her sister's demise. *I'm so sorry Katty.* She thought about Mia and tears started to fall. Two people that she cared about died from what she thought were no fault of their own.

The baby began to cry in the other room. She ignored him and continued to think about her dead loved ones. A thought of Bunny standing in the room with the sheet around her popped in her head and made her stomach churn. That's when she made the decision that Kevin and Nelson where going to be the first to go. She just had to find the right person to help her carry it out. The baby's cries became louder. *I wish he would shut the fuck up! Maybe I should have just let Ms. Gibbs take him.* Her patience was wearing thin with him. She didn't have time to play the mommy role. She noticed the baby got quiet all of a sudden. *I hope that lil fucker didn't stop breathing.* She ain't have time for D.F.S to get involved. She hopped up from the floor and went into the room.

"Oh shit!" Her heart almost jumped out of her chest. B.I was sitting on the bed holding the baby looking at him oddly. Nyse walked over to him and wrapped her arms around him and gave him a kiss.

"Baby, I missed you so much! I needed you. So much has happened! My brother tried to kill me but hit Mia instead. I'm so sorry, I know you loved her."

B.I cut her off. "I know…Uh this your son?" He had an odd look on his face. Nyse wasn't too sure what that was all about.

"Yeah, I told you I had a son. That's cool right?" She let go of him and stood back.

B.I continued to stare the baby in the face. It was almost as if he was looking through him.

"What's his dads name again?"

Nyse now had a stupefied look on her face. "Kevin. I told you that before. Why what's up?"

"Kevin…Kevin who?" He inquired.

All of his questions were starting to get on her nerves. *What is he trying to get at? I know he don't know my mom or brother because not many people know the truth.*

She became defensive. "Kevin Brockman, they call him Brock, he's from Northside. He gotta crazy ass sister who calls herself Fatal. I know you have to know her. From what I've seen, all them seem to have the same attributes. Uh let's see, I gotta brother named Nelson that tried to kill me and blames me for my sister Queen Kat's death. She and her sorry ass boyfriend Rashawn! Now tell me about you? You want to sit and question me like I don't know who the fuck my baby's dad is, how about you? What's up with you disappearing and being so fucking secretive all the time?" She yelled. She was fired up and breathing heavy.

B.I laid the baby down on the bed and began to rub the hair on his chin as he registered everything he was just told. He nodded his head and bit his lip.

"You said the dudes sister name was Fatal huh? The baby's cute though, he reminds me of someone that meant a lot to me. So, your *brother* killed my girl Mia huh? That's crazy. What we gonna do about that?" He extended his arms for Nyse to come to him. She sat on his lap.

"I don't know, baby, but we gotta do something. He gotta a lot of money now since Ra died. He left everything to him. For all I know he may have a hit out on me. That's why I've been laying low and staying here."

"This dude Ra must have thought a lot of your brother to leave him an empire."

Nyse nodded. "Yeah, he was going to marry my sister but some other shit happened. I don't really want to talk about it because it's still new for me. Since Mia died, all the emotions I had a few months ago during my sister's death is coming back. I just need to get away. Shit just ain't right. My son's father is on some other shit too. He's messing with the same chick my brother is messing with. I really don't care because he can sleep with whomever he wants to. I just don't like the fact that he had my baby over there trying to play house. I'm not going back to his house and he'll never see this baby again. It's not like he has any *real* say anyway."

B.I listened carefully to everything she said. "Why don't he have no say if that's his son?'

Nyse stood up and walked to the other side of the room. She sat down at the desk and sulked. B.I just stared at her. Then back at the baby. He knew she was lying about something. He was just waiting for her to tell him the truth. He laid back on the bed and played with the baby.

• •

Kevin sat outside of Aunt Bumpies Restaurant waiting for Fae to come out. When she did, she had two platters in her hand. She opened the door to Kevin's rental. "Hey lil brother! What's up with the rental?" She opened up her box of food and began to tear into the collard greens. Kevin sat and watched her eat like a grown ass man. He waited for her to hand him the second platter.

"Damn, can I get my food? I wanna eat too... shit!" He joked.

Fae put her fork down and squinted her eyes. "Nigga, where you got food at? I ain't get you nothing! This my shit. A bitch hungry!"

Kevin started his car and looked at her in amazement. "That's why your ass is gonna get big as a fuckin' house eating like that. I hope you choke on a chicken bone too!" He said playfully.

Fae laughed with him. "So you never answered my question. What's up with this rental? Where's ya truck?" She said with a mouth full.

"Man, that bitch done lost her fuckin' marbles. She had the balls to flatten all of my tires, then she torched my shit!"

Fae began to cough choking on her food. Kevin pulled over and slapped her on the back. Food came through her nose and mouth. "Oh shit, who torched your shit? I know Nyse ain't do it!" She said trying to get herself together.

Kevin laughed. "Yeah Nyse. Who else?"

Fae grinned. "Why? I know you fucked her up!"

Kevin turned at the red light heading to Lea Blvd. "I took my son with me while I was chillin' with my old head. Her daughter wanted to take the bay outside, I ain't see nothing wrong with it, so I let her take him. Not even 15 minutes later Nyse comes over ranting and raving and fucked my shit up. I wanted so bad to slide that bitch but I ain't trying to show my new chick the other side, ya know. So I went home that night to fuck her up but she was gone. You know I can't let her go just yet. I need her so I can get at her brother. What really took the cake was she bounced with my son and I ain't seen that bitch since. She even left her truck at the crib, so she got to be local. She be hanging over on the Ave. I ride through there on the regular trying to spot her but no luck."

"As in Concord Ave?" She inquired.

"Yeah, Concord Ave. She was hanging at the spot your boy be at. I just hope they haven't crossed paths because you know that will fuck everything up for us."

Fae didn't like that one bit. She knew what type of niggas Nyse was drawn too and if she meets up with him it's over.

"Lil bro, I think you may have to forget about that Nelson shit. You know he tried to kill her the night of her birthday? She called me begging me to kill him because he shot at her."

Kevin pulled into Colony North where he rented an apartment. This was where he handled all of his business.

He sat quietly for a moment trying to get his thoughts together. Then it all came to him. *Ain't this some shit? Mia. That's how she got killed?*

Fae studied his face she knew something was wrong. "What's up honey?"

"The junkie who your boy stays with, her daughter got shot that night. She must have been there with Nyse. My girl was there too and got hit with a bottle in the face. When Nyse saw her the day she torched my shit, she went off like she knew her. I guarantee that Nyse is the one who threw that damn bottle. I just need to know why." He put the car in reverse and headed towards 24th street.

● ●

Bunny poured the spaghetti noodles into the boiling water. She sang along with Aaliyah. *'If your girl only knew... that you was trying... to kick it with me...'* She was on cloud nine. Things were going great between her and Brock. Her bandages where off and her scar was hideous but she covered with her hair. He promised her that after it completely healed he would take her to the best plastic surgeon in the tri-state area. Tonight she planned on telling him everything she knew about Stack and what his next move against him was. She hadn't heard from him since the night he left her at the club. She had something for his ass.

She was a little noid. She wasn't sure how Brock would take the fact that she was fucking Stack but that was the past. When she told him what information she had, she was sure he would quickly get over it. She stirred the ground beef and added ketchup and tomato sauce. She heard the front door jingling. She checked the clock. It was only 4pm and her daughter caught the train to the Gallery to go school shopping, so she wouldn't be back for a while. Brock had to go handle some business and she doubted if he would be back already. She turned the heat down on the meat. She went down the hall towards the door and it opened. Brock came through followed by Fae.

"Hey baby…your home early."

She kissed him on the lips and turned her attention to the female. She was very petite, brown skin and very stylish with her gear. She looked as if she was some type of businesswoman. Bunny smiled warmly.

"Hi, how are you?" Fae gave her a half smile and brushed passed her.

"Babe, I need to talk to you for minute can you come in here?"

Bunny went into the living room and sat down on the couch next to Kevin.

"What's up, sweetie?"

"Look, I need to know everything that happened that night at the club. Don't leave anything out. I'm not gonna get mad, I just need you to be honest."

Bunny turned her attention to Fae. "Baby who's she?"

"I'm his sister, that's all you need to know." She said sarcastically. Fae didn't like her already. She saw right through her and knew she was up to something.

Bunny felt pressured she wanted to tell him but not like this. She took a deep breath and told them everything. Even the fact that she knew Kevin wasn't the baby's biological father. When she was finished she was relieved. She smelt a burning odor coming from the kitchen. She jumped up and ran into the kitchen. Her meat and noodles where burnt to a crisp. She took the pan and threw it into the sink. She was pissed. Kevin came in to see what was going on. He saw that she was upset. He went over to her and kissed her on the neck.

"It's cool, I just need you to be honest with me at all times. I hate liars…remember that. Thanks for telling me about Stack. You did good."

Fae watched the two of them at the door. *He ain't no damn different than Rashawn's ass. At least Rashawn knew Kat and Nyse. This nigga ain't know this broad from a can of paint.* Fae thought Kevin walked past her.

"Your ready, sis?" Fae rolled her eyes and followed him out.

A FATAL ATTRACTION

CHAPTER 20

So Lonely

"Your total is $252.39. Will that be cash or charge?" The young black cashier smiled cheerfully with her Santa Clause hat on.

It was Black Friday and Toys R Us was packed. B.I took Nyse out to buy the baby's Christmas gifts. They had been living together in Milford, Delaware in the Silver Lake apartments for the last three months. At first Nyse loved it. She was away from everybody and had time to think out her plans without interruption. She also thought this would be a chance to get to know B.I better. But she was still clueless. The only thing she knew was that he could lay great pipe and he treated her well. B.I still disappeared from time to time but nowhere near as much as he used too. When he wasn't around Corey would come down and spend time with her. Most of the time she wished he kept his ass up top though. He constantly nagged her about when he could come out with the information he knew. She wished he never told him anything because he was racking her nerves.

B.I handed the cashier the money with one hand while he held 7 month old Kevin who he nicknamed "man-man" in the other hand. To Nyse's surprise he was very good with him and treated him as if he was his own son. Nyse had begun to warm up to him a little better too. She had no choice. B.I would go off when she acted anything less than a perfect mother to him. Yesterday was Thanksgiving and they spent it alone. B.I went to go visit a sick relative. Nyse wanted to ask him who it was but he would shut down on her whenever she questioned

K.D. Harris   125

him about anything concerning his past. He would always tell her he didn't think she was ready for his truth. She would always drop the conversation because with him it was a no win situation.

Nyse pushed the cart to his car and opened the trunk. B.I placed the baby in the car seat and strapped him in. She waited for him to unlock the doors so she could get inside. Jealousy overcame her. She was starting to get fed up.

"Damn, you treat that nigga better than me. What you fuckin' him or something?"

B.I shut the baby's door. Went around the side of the car and unlocked the door. When Nyse got in he punched her dead in the mouth. She held her mouth and cried. That wasn't the first time she was hit by him but it was usually right before sex. That was their new thing. He would sometimes pretend that he was raping her. At first she thought it was crazy but later she learned to love it. This time, however, was different. They weren't about to get into a session.

"Don't you ever say no sick shit like that again." He started the car and pulled off.

"Sorry B., I just think you care more about the baby than me. Kevin did that shit too I just don't understand how y'all can be so into a baby that ain't even yours."

B.I slowed the car down and turned to her and gave her a look as to say *you done fucked up*. Nyse knew she messed up she turned her head and looked out the passenger window. She sighed deeply and decided to come clean.

"Kevin is not Lil Kevin's father. His real dad is dead. His name was Rashawn Gibbs. The one I told you was killed along with my sister. And my ex-boyfriend Spinx was killed with them. Rashawn was going to marry my sister, Kat. Before you judge me, let me tell you my side."

She told him the story she told everyone that Rashawn raped her. B.I was attentive and didn't interrupt her.

"So I was at the hotel with Spinx. I went to the bathroom and the front door of the room opened. It was Fatal and my sister. I was

126

scared so I hid in the linen closet. Then Rashawn came into the room. Everyone was arguing. That's when I found out that Ra and Fae had also been fucking. My sister started snapping and Fatal shot her in the head. I tried to stop her but it was too late. Then Rashawn attacked Fatal and she sliced his throat. By that time, Spinx rushed me out the room. That's when we ran into Kevin in the parking garage and Fatal killed Spinx. It was all a set up. I was just a pawn in their sick game." Nyse broke down in tears.

B.I stared straight ahead and drove home without saying a word.

• •

Two weeks went by since Nyse told B.I the truth about Lil Kevin. He seemed to grow closer to the baby and hadn't left their side. Nyse tried to keep her distance from the two. She stayed in her room and smoked most of the time. She thought he was mad at her for lying. Their sex didn't stop but he seemed to be more aggressive than ever with her. It was to the point it was straight painful and she wasn't enjoying it anymore. She found herself wanting to go back to Wilmington. She was bored. All she did was get high all the time and eat. She had gotten up to a size 10 and she wasn't feeling that at all. She made her mind up. She was getting the hell out of there ASAP.

The next morning she and B.I were laying in the bed. She laid her head on his chest like she always did and played with his hairs. "Baby, you awake?"

He didn't answer her. "I wanna leave. I can't stay here anymore. This shit is starting to get the best of me. I'm not built for this country shit. I know I can't break the lease but you can stay here. I got money to pay for the remainder of the time we have on it."

B.I sat up in the bed. "You wanna leave me?"

Nyse sat up next to him. "No…we can go back up there together. Your good to me. I just don't like the fact that I don't know anything about you. I been fucking with you for damn near six months and I don't even know your real name."

"Eric…"

"Huh?" She questioned.

"My real name is Eric, B.I is a nick name my mother gave me. It stands for bad influence. We didn't really get along all that well, ya know. I had a little brother and she didn't want me around him because she thought my attitude would rub off on to him. So one day he got into some shit and she blamed me. We argued and she told me to leave. I wouldn't so she stabbed me right here." He pointed to the scar on his neck. "I ran out the house and drove myself to Wilmington hospital. The knife was still inside me. I didn't want to remove it and do more damage. I hadn't talked to my mother again. She called me not too long ago before she got sick but I didn't respond until it was too late." Nyse kissed him softly.

"Baby, I'm so sorry…just know that she's in a better place now." She said sincerely.

"What happened to your little brother? She asked.

"I'm not sure, man-man reminds me so much of him I guess that's why I take to him."

Nyse smiled warmly. "Well I hope everything works out for you and you don't have to worry about losing us." She snickered. "But I still want to get the hell away from here."

"That's cool we'll leave right after the holidays. I need to handle some shit up there anyway."

Nyse smiled slyly. *So do I.*

• •

It was Christmas day. Fae decided to spend the day with Kevin and his new family. She still didn't like Bunny but she promised Kevin she would behave for his sake. She watched as Bunny opened up another jewelry box. She pulled out a platinum bracelet and necklace with a ruby and diamond heart. *This shit is sickening.* She wanted to throw up at the sight of the two. They were always kissing and touching all over each other. *He must really be into this bitch. He was-n't like that with Nyse.*

Speaking of Nyse, Fae wondered where the hell she disap-peared too. She hadn't seen or heard from her in over 3 months. She and Kevin had been looking for her. It's like she and the baby disap-peared into thin air. She changed her cell number and everything. What bothered Kevin was the fact that she left everything including her car. He thought she was over on the Ave. but no one over there had seen her either. She wasn't the only one who pulled a disappearing act. Her brother Stacks was laying low also. She knew he was still around because his business was still flowing. So he had to be somewhere, just highly protected.

Fae still talked to Eric from time to time. He wasn't around as much anymore which was good. He would only came up to visit his mother who was still in a coma. She didn't understand why he just didn't pull the plug already. The woman was brain dead. He was just paying to keep her heart pumping. She was happy that everything went smoothly with Caree so the heat could be taken off of her. She wished to God that it was Nyse hanging from that rope burning but she knew she would be hanging right next to her. When Nyse did pop back up she promised to make her die a slow painful death. Her tak-ing that baby was tearing Kevin apart, he tried not to show it, but Fae knew her brother. She looked underneath the tree and there were a bunch of toys for no other than Lil Kev.

Fae wanted to smack some sense into him and tell him to get over it but it was no sense in that. Kevin still had hope that he was going to get him back.

CHAPTER 21

Setting Things In Order

"Baby, I missed you so much. It feels so good to be up in you again." Nyse was on all fours with her head buried in the pillow while Corey drilled deep inside her. She enjoyed every stroke as he massaged her ass.

"I missed you too, baby." Nyse moaned.

Corey picked up speed and let out all of his love juices inside of her. He nibbled up the spine of her back then collapsed next to her. Nyse rolled over and crawled into his arms.

Nyse hadn't even been back a full 24 hours before she found herself laid up at the Fairfield Inn with Corey. She and the baby moved into an apartment complex out Newark called "The Village of Windover." It was no School Bell but it would do. B.I went out of town to handle his business. The baby was now going to daycare, so Nyse had her days to herself until 6:30pm. That still didn't give her enough time to do what she had to do but the complex was filled with teenage girls. It would be no time before she had one of them watching him.

"Baby, It's January now and you still haven't given me the ok to go ahead to tell my superior's what I know. I'm trying to be patient but I may have to just tell. You know I'm breaking the law by withholding information."

Nyse sighed and got out of the bed. "Man, you would fuck up a wet dream! We sitting here spending time enjoying ourselves and you bring up your sorry ass job. Is that the only reason why you fuck with me? So you can get information to further your career?" Nyse questioned.

"Baby, no That's not it at all." He walked over to her and held her tightly. She broke away from him.

"I can't tell! It seems like every time we are together you bring it up and I'm fucking tired of it. If you feel as though you have to get your super cop award, go right ahead and handle your business. Just make sure you tell my son you're the reason why his mom ended up dead because you wanted to be top cop!"

She stormed into the bathroom and locked the door her face was flushed. She felt her cheeks and they were hot. She wasn't feeling that well. She had been feeling bad for the last few days. She didn't know what was up. She felt her stomach get queasy and suddenly she bent over the toilet and vomited. Corey stood by the door. He heard her getting sick.

"Baby, let me in…you ok? He jiggled the doorknob.

"No I'm not alright. You're stressing me the fuck out!" She felt more coming up. She bent down again and more vomit came pouring out her mouth. Her stomach was empty so nothing came up but clear liquids.

When she was finally finished she rinsed her mouth out and brushed her teeth. She opened the door and Corey took hold of her hand. "I can't…I need to lie down." She told him. He let her go and followed her back to the bed. He tucked her under the covers and laid next to her.

"You alright, baby?"

"Yeah, I just need you to stop badgering me. I promise you that you gonna be in a good position if you just let me do what I got to do." She laid quietly getting her thoughts together while he held her tightly. "I may have some information that you can release. I just don't know how it would benefit you because it's out of your jurisdiction."

"It doesn't matter as long as long as it's in New Castle County I'm good." He gave her his full attention.

"My brother Nelson is pushing cocaine to just about every drug dealer in the city. He stays at my sister's old house in Newark. Downstairs in the basement there's a secret compartment along the paneling under the steps. That's where my sister used to keep large sums of money. I guarantee you'll find something in there. My brother's an asshole. He's not smart at all. Rashawn had a safe house over on the west side, two doors down from his mother on 8th and Scott. I doubt if anything has changed and more importantly, remember the girl Mia Snow? She got shot in the head at the Safari back in August. I was with her and that bullet was intended for me but hit her instead. Nelson was the one who pulled the trigger. I'm pretty sure he's still on probation too, so he should be easy to find." Nyse informed.

Corey was elated he wanted to jump out of the bed and click his heels together. That was music to his ears. *Fuck being a Lt! Shit, I might run for Mayor of Wilmington! They would love me if I single handedly shut down a major trade.*

"Thank you, baby. I love you." He kissed her shoulder

Nyse rolled over and closed her eyes. *I bet. One down, two more to go.*

• •

The next morning Nyse dropped the baby off early at daycare. She had a full day ahead of her. She needed to go to the hair salon she found in Bear, Delaware called Mink. When she used to live out in Serenity Hills, a few girls used to go and get their hair done there. She needed a new look. Her face had filled out, so she wanted something vibrant and shorter. While she sat in the stylist chair she made a call to a friend she hadn't spoken to in months. The phone just rang until the answering machine came on. *I guess he's not going to answer because he doesn't know the number.* She decided to pop up on him.

An hour later the stylist handed her the mirror. "Wow! This doesn't even look like me!" She exclaimed. The stylist wasn't sure if that was a compliment or not.

"Do you like it?" She asked nervously.

"Like it, honey? I love it! It's so bouncy and sooo.... ravishing.... ravishing red!" She said sounding like a Dark and Lovely hair care commercial. Her hair was cut right above her shoulders and styled in a wet set. She had it dyed a bright red and it fit her perfectly. Nyse thought the color gave her an edge and she was feeling it to the fullest.

She paid the stylist and gave her a generous tip. She got into her rented Chrysler Sebring. She was tired of having to get rental's she wanted to get her truck but she wasn't quite ready for Kevin to know she was back. She looked at the sky and noticed it had a grey over tone. Snow wasn't in the forecast but from the looks of it, they were in for a bad storm. She popped in one of B.I's M.O.P CD's and put on her favorite track. *Firing Squad.*

She rode to Wilmington and decided to take I-495. She was going to take the Market street way to get to 27th and Tatnall. She didn't want to run into anyone who might recognize her. She turned on to 30th and Market and circled around until she was on 26th and Tatnall. She rode slowly down the street in search of Jab or someone that knew him. She stopped at the stop sign and someone tapped on her passenger side window. Nyse jumped. There was a guy bundled up in a bright yellow Pelle coat. She was about to peel off but something told her not too. She rolled down the window just enough to hear him speak. "Yo, what you need?" he asked.

She sucked her teeth in repulsion. "Mother fucker do I look like I want to buy some bullshit drugs?"

The guy pulled the facemask down to get a closer look at her. "Oh shit, you're the crazy broad from the Safari." He started cracking up laughing.

Nyse didn't see what was so amusing.

"Do I know you?"

"Bitch, don't act like you don't remember. Your ass was ass naked running down Lancaster. You thought we wanted to rape your yella ass! Ain't nobody wanna rape you. After a few minutes with me you would have been begging for me to give you some of this monster." He said in arrogance. Nyse turned her nose up. She remembered exactly who he was. He was the dude that was sitting next to her in the back. Jab's little brother.

Nyse rolled her eyes. "Honey, please I ain't never begged for no dick and don't plan too. Besides your lame ass wouldn't last two minutes with a bitch of my caliber! Anyway where's Jab?"

"Why you looking for Jab? You should be saying where's Littlez." He said with cockiness.

"Who the fuck is a Littlez?"

"You looking at him, Bitch. The one and only." He said admiring himself.

"Littlez huh? I bet your name fits you perfectly?" She said sarcastically.

He decided to give up he liked her style but he could see he would have to go back and forth with her for hours in order to get the last word.

"Man, shut the fuck up and park your bullshit Sebring over there." He pointed to a space on the corner.

Nyse laughed. She parked the car and walked over towards him. He took her into a house two doors down from where he was standing. Once inside they both removed their coats. She held her Mink jacket in her hand. He threw his coat across the chair. She got a look at him. He was chocolate tall and a little stocky. Both wrists were iced up and he had a platinum necklace with an iced out Jesus piece. *Flashy and arrogant.* Nyse shook her head.

"You can have a seat. I'mma go get him for you.

A few minutes later they both came back down the steps. Jab looked the same. He had his dreds pulled back into a ponytail. She stood up and gave him a hug.

"Damn girl, I thought you fell off the face of the earth. Your dude has the FBI, CIA, and every damn body else hunting your ass down. Where you been?" He sat on the couch next to her.

"I needed some time to get my thoughts together. As for

134

Brock, Kevin or whatever you call him, I'm done with his ass. But I'm sure y'all already know that. I know y'all seen him with his new thing. I ain't making no noise about that bitch, she can't hold a match to me anyway. But enough about that, I wanna talk business."

Jab looked at his brother and they both smiled. "Business, what do you know about talking business?"

"Nyse crossed her legs and sat back on the couch. "Honey, behind this beauty is brains. I know more than I let on. I know that Stack and his crew is about to get shut the fuck down within the next week or so. If you fucking with him you need to stop. I also know that Kevin's connect is in Atlanta and he's knockin' y'all in the head big time." She pulled a phone number out of her Coach bag.

"This right here is Kevin's connect. I already called him and told him that he should be expecting a call and he promised to treat y'all real nice."

"So what's in it for you?" Jab asked.

"Nothing, let's just say it's a gift of appreciation for looking out for me in a time of need. By the way, Kevin has a stash house in Colony North. The address is on the back of the paper. I'll be in touch." She stood up and gave Jab a hug. Littlez stood up too. They both looked at each other and rolled their eyes. Jab laughed but she gave him a hug just for the hell of it.

"You couldn't wait to get your hands around all of this. I know you felt my pole ready to rip straight through you?" He said laughing. Nyse gave him the finger and left out the door. *Two down one more to go.*

CHAPTER 22

It's Going Down

"Excuse me Miss, uhh you're gonna have to turn your car around. This is a crime scene." The officer was directing traffic because the Westside was on lock. From 5th and Madison all the way up to 8th and Scott Street.

"What's going on, sir?" Fae asked.

"Watch the 6'o-clock news. Right now you have to get out of here your blocking traffic."

Fucking Pig. Fae made a U-turn in the middle of Fourth street and went towards the Eastside. She picked up the phone and called Eric. He didn't answer. She left him a message.

"Hey, the cops got everything blocked off. Something is going on up there so you just gonna have to meet me at my crib." She hung up and called Kevin.

He picked up on the first ring. "Yo, something major just happened over on the west. It's jump out vans, the fucking ATF and some more shit over here you know anything about it?"

"That nigga Stacks just got popped! They ran up in his crib in Newark, you know Kat's old crib. They found guns, a fews Kilo's and money. That nigga had been staying there the whole time. They said when they ran up in there he was laid up with some chick. That lil nigga was still on probation so you know he ain't never seeing the light of day unless he snitch." Kevin was hyped.

"Damn that's crazy. I wonder if one of those guns was the one he used to kill that girl. I hope for his sake he was smart enough to get rid of it." Fatal stated.

"Man, I don't know. But look let me make this call. I called my connect and that nigga ain't returning my calls. I hope shit is right with him. I don't know what I'm gonna do now since Stacks is out the picture. It's gonna be a drought now. Hold on Fae, that's my other line."

Fae waited for a minute on hold. She was about to hang up until she heard him yelling hysterically.

"What's wrong?!" She said alarmed.

"That was the fucking property manager from my apartment! Somebody broke into my shit! Meet me over there now!" He hung up the phone.

"What the fuck is going on today?" She said out loud and made her way to Colony North.

• •

Fae ran up to Kevin's old apartment he was already there searching through his things. Everything was gone including his money, coke, weed, and even his porno's. Fae looked around and the place was ransacked.

"Damn they fucked this shit up! Is everything gone?" Kevin was close to tears.

"They ain't leave shit, not even my toothpaste, nothing is here. This can't be fucking happening. I ain't got nothing left. I got 10g's in the safe at the other house but all my big money was here. They took over $70k in cash and another 50 in drugs. I'mma have to start all over again. I'm broke." He sat on the couch and cried.

Fae was hot. "Kevin stop that shit! Don't cry you a fucking man! You don't cry over nothing like this. We gonna get your shit back. Delaware is only but so big. Somebody's gonna talk. We just have to sit back and watch which niggas start flossin' extra hard and tell on their fucking self. Then I'mma finish them. Have you noticed anyone following you around or anyone acting suspicious all of a sudden?"

Kevin thought about it for a minute. "Naw, I ain't been really in the streets like that Roc has been handling everything. I've been spending most of my time with Bunny. Damn Bunny."

Fae's radars went up. "What? You think she had something to do with it?"

"Naw, we find out if she's pregnant or not today. If she was pregnant I was gonna put money down on this town house out Frenchtown Woods. I ain't want to raise my baby in the city."

Fae couldn't believe what she was hearing. *Pregnant? Buy a house? Next this nigga will be talking about marrying that Ho!* She had to put a stop to this shit. It was time for Bunny to go.

"So you think she's pregnant? Are you sure it's yours?"

He shot her a disturbing glance. "Are you serious? Of course it's mine! Who else's would it be? I'm with her damn near 24 hours a day!" Kevin explained.

"No need to get hostile I just asked you a simple question. It's just kind of ironic that Stacks get popped and your shit gets ran up in all in the same day and you both have one thing in common...Bunny." She said trying to make a point. Kevin sat silent rubbing his temples trying to think. He knew Fae had a point but he doubted very much if Bunny would do anything like that. She had no reason to harm him because he was taking care of her and her daughter. Then it came to him.

"I really don't think that Bunny is capable of pulling something off like this but we both know who is vindictive enough to and has enough information on me and Stacks to pull it off."

They looked at each other and in unison said, "Nyse!"

• •

Nyse sat on the bench facing the Caesar Rodney statue at Rodney Square. The weather was too mild for it to be February. She

138

looked at her watch and noticed it was 11am. *If he's not here in 10 minutes I'm outta here.* Even though it would be hard to recognize her at first glance she didn't want to take any chances.

Rodney Square was packed as always because it was the main spot to catch public transportation. Every Dart bus in New Castle County stopped here. Today was worse because the whole Westside was shut down thanks to Nyse. She had a front row seat watching it all go down compliments of Corey. He called her last night to inform her that they were running up in her sister's old house at 6am that morning. She set her alarm so she could be there when it went down. She parked her car at the Acme market across the road. She had on her work out gear to blend in with the rest of the morning joggers and walkers that used the track at the local high school.

Being there allowed her to get a perfect view of the house. At 5:30am she was on the track pretending to warm up. At 6am on the dot, she heard a big boom and trucks helicopters and agents came from everywhere. Everyone stopped and watched. Nyse stayed long enough to see them pull Stacks out in handcuffs. That's all she needed to see. She left feeling victorious. At 9am she received a call from Jab asking her to meet him somewhere.

"Every time I see you look different!" Jab came up behind her startling her a little. Nyse stood up to greet him. She ran her hands through her bone straight her. "It's still the same. I just straightened it out that's all." They both sat down.

"So what's up?"

"I'll tell you what's up. Thanks to you I'mma whole lot richer. Everything went smoothly with the new connect. We cleared your boy out last night. He was really holding out on a nigga."

Nyse shook her head. "I told you he was working y'all. But you could have told me all of this on the phone you ain't have to drag me out in the cold. Unless you just wanted to see my beautiful face." She teased.

Jab smiled. "Naw you cool as shit, but your ass is dangerous. I would have to kill your ass if you ever did the shit you just pulled on ole' boy to me." He half joked.

Nyse knew he meant what he was saying and she was cool with it. She couldn't take on another dude. It would just detour her from accomplishing her last goal. Plus it was hard enough juggling Corey and B.I. Her body seemed to be breaking down. She was tired all the time. She needed to go get vitamins.

He pulled a brown paper bag out of his pocket along with a wrapped gift and handed it to her. "I know you said you ain't want shit but this is just a token of our appreciation."

She gave him a hug and then opened the gift box." She pulled out a platinum chain with a diamond encrusted medallion with the word "Poison" written in pink diamonds across it and a snake with ruby eyes. It was hot as hell. Nyse admired it but didn't know how she should feel about it. Jab noticed she was having mixed emotions.

"You don't like it?" He asked surprised.

Nyse gasped. "I love it! I just don't know if I should take this as a compliment or a diss." She laughed. "I know you didn't buy this."

He laughed. "Naw, that's a gift from Littlez. You know he's all about flash. But seriously, you should take that as a compliment ain't nothing wrong with knowing how to handle yourself." She gave him a hug.

"Littlez huh? It figures! Could you put this on for me?" She asked.

He put the necklace around her neck and clasped it. She opened the bag and saw that it was a stack of money.

"Don't count that shit out here. It's $15k, I know it ain't much but if you ever need me I'm just a phone call away. Me and my people's are gonna lay low for a minute. I don't wanna draw no attention. Ya know?"

She agreed they both said their goodbyes and went their separate ways. Nyse looked down at her necklace and it beamed. *Poison...I think I like that.*

CHAPTER 23

Gigs Up

I wonder where that sneaky bitch is hiding? Fae poured herself a cup of coffee and added her usual amount of Hennessey. She took a sip and it stung her throat as it went down. She put two pieces of Raisin bread in the toaster and sat at her breakfast bar to enjoy her meal.

Yesterday's news Journal was still sitting in the same spot she left it in. Nelson Nyse's picture was splattered across the front page. Just about his whole crew got popped. They had pictures displaying all the drugs, weapons and money that they found in several locations. On page two, there was a full-page article on the officer Corey Hamilton who organized the whole sting operations.

Fatal studied his picture. He was handsome, somewhat distinguished looking. "I wonder what little birdie was on your window seal." She thought out loud. There was no way he figured all this out without some help from a reliable source. A source she believed he was probably sleeping with. No other than little Ms. Nalyse Nyse herself. She took another sip of her drink. *Fucking Rat.* She tolerated a lot but she loathed a fucking snitch.

In her mind they should not only have their tongues cut out but also their eyes should be burned out of their heads and their ears cut off. That way they won't see, hear and won't be able to tell shit. There were too many other ways to skin a cat other than snitching. To her, that was the cowardly and easy way out. *That bitch is devious! I know she could have found a better way to hang him.* She knew that Nelson wasn't built for the Feds so she knew he was going to do a whole lot of talking and Wilmington wasn't going to be the same for a minute. Too many people would be too scared to move anything. She stretched and yawned. *Well looks like I'm back in business.*

The upside of this was she would get crazy business. Certain people would pay top dollar to makes sure that Nelson and whoever else that needed to be dealt with wouldn't make it to court. That made a smile appear on her face. She missed working. She was tired of sitting around Kevin and his makeshift family. That nigga was so pussy whipped it wasn't funny. The look on Bunny's face was unforgettable when he told her he was damn near broke. That bitches black heart fell to pieces. She looked like she wanted to cry. Kevin tried to console her and she acted as if she didn't want to touch him. That's when she decided that when the time was right Bunny's journey would be coming to an abrupt end whether Kevin liked it or not. He would get over it just like he got over all the others.

Her doorbell rang interrupting her thoughts. She looked at the clock on the wall and it read 8:30 am. *I wonder who would be coming here this early?* It could only be a handful of people because not many people knew where she resided. She looked through the peephole. *Eric?* She opened the door.

"Hey, I forgot we were meeting today...come on in." He entered and took a seat at her dining room table.

"Eric sit on the couch, it's more comfortable." She directed him.

He had a perplexed look on his face. "I'm not staying long. I just wanted to tell you that my mom died this morning."

Fae grabbed her chest and sat next to him. "I'm so sorry Eric. Is there anything you want me to do?"

"Naw, ain't nothing nobody can do now. I'm at peace with it. I just wanted the person who did that to her to pay and *you* made that possible. I think you've done the ultimate don't *you* think so?" He raised his eyebrow and bit on his lip, he was gazing into her eyes.

Fae knew what he was trying to do. She gave him complete eye contact. She dared not to look away. That would be a death sentence. "I would do anything for you, Eric. I owe you my life. I don't know what would have happened to me if it weren't for you." Fae sincerely admitted.

Eric nodded. "I appreciate that. Now since mom is gone, I can venture on to my next mission."

Fae was ecstatic to hear that. *Good he's ready to roll the fuck out for good!* "I understand that. I know that Delaware brings you a lot of bad memories especially with Rashawn and your mom being gone now. Besides me, there's nothing really keeping you here." She said full of hope. He played with the hair on his chin as she talked.

"You gotta point. If that was entirely true. I still have family here, my nephew. My mother called me right after Ra's death and said he had a little boy. That the baby's mom was keeping her away from him. She said she had this other nigga raising him and even gave him his name. You know whose name she told me?"

Fae's body stiffened. She looked towards the kitchen drawer where she kept her gun. There was no way she would be able to retrieve it without Eric knowing what was up. She knew he was carrying. *This is not happening.* She didn't want anything to happen to Kevin but she wasn't losing her life over anyone. It was finally being revealed that the child being raised as her nephew was actually his.

She kept calm as possible. She knew she couldn't let him see her sweat. "Enlighten me." She said straight-faced.

"No need too. You already know. I just want my nephew back and no harm will come to your precious brother." He said calmly. "I need to ask you a question. Are you sure that girl you killed was the right one who murdered my mother? I could have sworn she was trying to tell me something before you set her on fire. That shit has been bothering me since and shit don't usually fuck with me."

"Eric, you heard for yourself! She admitted it. I had a reliable source that said that she did it. Are you questioning my loyalty to you now? I would never cross you. I'm not crazy!" She jumped from her seat and towards the kitchen. Her behavior became erratic. She was losing it and Eric had her right where he wanted her.

He met her in the kitchen and grabbed her by her arms. "Baby, calm down. I'm just asking some questions and you're falling apart. Is there something bothering you?"

"No, I'm fine. Kevin doesn't have your nephew he's with the mother. I don't know where she is and neither does Kevin. He just used to sell to her ex. I guess when that shit happened with Kevin she just threw the baby on him since everyone thought he was dead. There was no way he could defend himself but I have no idea how to find them."

Eric let her go. He couldn't believe that of all people Fatal, someone he once loved with all his heart, had betrayed him over some nut ass nigga who wasn't even her real brother. He was so angry inside that he wanted to snap her neck in two. He would play her little game for now but in the end she would pay with her life especially if Nyse was telling the truth about her killing Rashawn.

"So you won't find my nephew for me?"

"It's not that I won't I don't think I can. She disappeared without a trace. Shit she may already be dead. From what I heard the bitch is treacherous. She was hated by many. The most I can do is ask some of her old friends out the 'Hills'. Maybe she kept in touch with them." Fae looked away and started fidgeting with the dishwasher controls. Her nerves were getting the best of her and she needed her medicine to calm down.

"I'm about to go, but before I do I'm putting you on one more assignment and the words *no and I can't* will not be tolerated. I need you to find the person or person's who are responsible for my brother's death. Maybe then I'll have a clue to my nephew's whereabouts." With that he walked out the door before Fae could give any type of rebuttal.

She stood there stoned faced. For a minute she felt her heart drop. One single tear fell down her cheek. There was a kitchen knife lying on the counter. For a minute she contemplated suicide. She took the knife and held it against her juggler vein. *I can't go out like this.* She dropped the knife in the sink and for the first time in along time, she cried. She let it all come out. When she was done she retrieved her phone and dialed Kevin's phone number. He didn't pick up. She was furious. She was tired of not having his full attention. She made up her mind that this would be the last time he would leave her out in the cold.

CHAPTER 24

Kill the Bitch

Nyse laughed as she read the obituaries. *'On February 10th, Eliza Ann Gibbs went to be with the Lord. There will be a private ceremony at an undisclosed location.' It's undisclosed because ain't nobody gonna be there!* Nyse thought.

"Man-Man, your nasty ass mom-mom kicked the bucket." She told the baby as if he knew what she was talking about. He laughed and bounced up and down in his walker. "Go man-man, go man-man it's your birthday!" She sang.

The day started off great for Nyse the wicked witch of the west was dead. B.I had been gone for the last few days, Kevin was broke and Nelson was behind bars. Yesterday was Valentine's day and her and Corey went to the Cheesecake Factory and later he took her on a shopping Spree at King of Prussia. He and his wife had been having issues. So most of his time was now being spent with her. He hadn't been bugging her that much about the murders since he already made Lieutenant thanks to Nyse.

She was going out tonight. She was tired of sitting in the house. She was going to the *Thunder Guards* with her next-door neighbor. She had found a young girl in the neighborhood to watch the baby when she wanted to stay out. She looked in the full-length mirror at herself she was fly as always. She had on a pair of Baby Phat dark wash Jeans with a black fitted low cut baby Phat logo shirt. Her red hair was now cut in layers that fell towards her face giving her a Diva effect. To top it off, she put on her trademark necklace. *Bitches is gonna be hating.* She put on her mink vest and was out the door.

The line was out the door when they pulled up. "Damn, is it always crowded like this? She asked.

Her neighbor replied. "Umm-hmmm, it's because they don't close until like 4am so there ain't no where else to go in Delaware but here. Half the time nobody goes in. They just hang across the street at that vacant parking lot. I wanna go in though because I need to get my drink on." She opened the door and got out. "You comin?"

Nyse nodded. "Yeah give me a minute. I gotta make a phone call real quick." She lied.

When she was out of sight, she pulled out a blunt and sparked it. She didn't want everybody all up in her business. The girl was cool but not that damn cool. After she achieved the high she was looking for she entered the club. It was packed. All of Riverside and the Bucket were up in the place. She didn't know too many of them so she was comfortable. She sat at the bar and flirted with the old men who where actually apart of the motorcycle club. She heard that a few of the "Thunder Guards" were paid but old men where not her thang. She just talked shit and enjoyed the free drinks. After a few hours of that shit she grew tired and wanted to leave. She went on the dance floor to search for her girl but it was almost impossible. It was like looking for a needle in a haystack.

She didn't want to leave her but if she didn't pop up in the next few minutes she was out of there with or without her. She went to the area where the pool tables were and she found her all up in some nigga's face. She approached her.

"I'm about to roll out." The girl looked at her with pleading eyes. Nyse's eyes were half shut. She was feeling the herself. "Don't look at me like that. You better tell this nigga you all hugged up with to take you home."

"I'll make sure your girl gets home safely." He said. To Nyse it didn't matter anyway her mind was already made up, she was gone,

K.D. Harris   147

at least that was her plan.

• •

This is Déjà vu like a motherfucker. Bunny was sitting on her new conquests lap watching Nyse like a hawk. At first she wasn't sure if she was seeing correctly. The red hair and the extra weight she put on threw her off a bit but it was her. Nyse was back and she couldn't wait to tell Kevin. He had been looking for her for months and his search intensified over the last few weeks. His stash house was robbed and he knew Nyse had something to do with it especially since her brother went down around the same time.

Bunny didn't put anything past her especially after the dramatic display she put on in front of her house right before she disappeared. Bunny had to admit, she secretly admired her. She didn't know anyone who had enough nerve to set a nigga's shit on fire right before his eyes. If it weren't for her fucking her face up, she would have went over there and congratulated her for a job well done.

She walked a little closer to get a good look at her. She tried to be careful so she didn't see her. Bunny didn't want any confrontation in front of her new man. He didn't know she was still playing house with a nigga. She was just trying to figure out how to get rid of Kevin. Now since she was pregnant, it was going to be a little harder than expected. She had no use for him anymore. He didn't take over Stacks drug spots as planned. He didn't even have a stable connect anymore. That nigga was finished and so was she. She looked around and seemed to have lost sight of Nyse. She felt someone tapping her on the shoulder. She turned around and jumped back.

"So, we meet again." Nyse said slyly.

"Excuse me? I don't think I know you." Bunny tried to walk away but Nyse grabbed her.

"Bitch, don't play stupid you know who the fuck I am."

Bunny tried to play it off. "Oh my God…Nyse right? Sweetie,

148

if I were you I would go right back to the rock you crawled from under. The streets are talking honey and your name is quite popular and not in a positive way. So I suggest that you get to stepping and I'll keep your little secret." Before she walked off she added. "He don't need his *fake son* anymore because I'm pregnant with his *real* child."

Pregnant? I know this bitch ain't trying to play me. Without thinking twice Nyse grabbed a pool stick and wacked her upside her head. Bunny turned around and tried to grab at her but some big burley guy rushed Bunny knocking her to the floor. Nyse was able to make her way through the crowd to get to her. She took full advantage of her being on the floor. She stomped her in her stomach with the heel of her boot. She wanted to kick the life out of her. The crowd started to get rowdy and a few other fights broke out. A bouncer broke through the crowd and grabbed Nyse up and threw her across his shoulder. She tried to wiggle her way out of his grasp but it wasn't working. He had her locked down. Once they were outside he let her down and hurried back in to control the scene.

The police must have known something was going to jump off because they were speeding down Governor Pritz Blvd. Nyse staggered as she tried to get to her car. She wanted to make a clean get away before someone could point her out as the one who caused the ruckus.

• •

It must have been a full moon because the maternity triage unit at the Christian hospital was in full swing. It seemed as if everyone was about to drop their load. Fae sat in the lobby trying to console a distraught Kevin. He received a phone call from one of his boy's who witnessed the ass kicking Nyse had put on Bunny. He didn't believe him at first because Bunny wasn't supposed to be at the Thunder Guards. He had dropped her off at her mother's house in Burlington, NJ early that morning to spend the weekend with her family. How she ended up back in Wilmington he didn't know and how the hell she ran into Nyse was really a mind boggler. He had been searching for her for months and now she just pops up of all places the *Thunder Guards*. Everybody and their mother, *literally,* partied there. He took it as her trying to toy with him.

"Is there a Mr. Brockman out here?" A young black nurse announced. Kevin jumped to his feet and Fae followed closely behind him. They followed the nurse through double doors into the triage area.

"Is the baby ok?" He asked anxiously.

The nurse gave him a fake smile. "Sir, you would need to talk to her doctor about that. He should be in to speak to you both in a few. There are a few other patients ahead of you."

She opened the door to the room Bunny was in. Kevin rushed through the door and ran to be by Bunny's side. He didn't even hold the door like he would usually for Fae. She had to catch it before it slapped it in her face.

Her face grimaced at the sight of them being all lovey dovey. Bunny had a monitor strapped around her stomach to monitor the baby's heartbeat. She didn't understand how they could even pick up a heartbeat when she was only supposed to be two months pregnant. Fae pulled the chair up and sat on the opposite side. She didn't look beat up to her. She thought it was all bullshit. There weren't any bruises, no scratches, and her hair was still in place. Either Nyse couldn't fight a lick or this bitch made this shit up for attention.

"I thought Kevin dropped you off at your moms. How did you get back to Wilmington, and at the Guards of all places? You're pregnant why the fuck would you want to be at the club?" She ice grilled Bunny. Before she was able to speak she added, "How did you of all people, manage to run into a bitch that half of Wilmington has been looking for? That's fucking me up something crazy."

Bunny turned to Kevin for help. But he wasn't bailing her out of that one he wanted to know the answers as well. She closed her eyes and sighed.

"My girls from Burlington wanted to go out. We were supposed to go to Philly but she wanted to hang out in Delaware."

"So you take her to the *Guards*?" Fae interrupted. "That's like me telling my peoples who lives in B-more let's not go to Hammerjacks, let's go to The Kozy Korner. What sense does that shit make?"

Kevin jumped in. "Fae, give her a chance to explain."

"Well it doesn't even matter anyway, what does matter is she attacked me and I'm pregnant, I want to press charges." Bunny complained.

"Press charges? Honey, we don't do the police. We handle things our way. You're not pressing charges on anyone, that's snitchin'." Fae snapped.

Bunny was sick of Fae. She was tired of her always having a say in their business. What really burned her up was that Kevin never stood up to her. She felt her blood boiling. This was going to stop. She was a grown ass woman and she didn't care what type of reputation Fae had. If she tried anything she would have her ass locked up quicker than she could blink. What Fae didn't know was Kevin opened up to Bunny and told her damn near everything there was to know about Fae. He even told her the fact that Fae killed her own mother. He had her swear that she would never breathe a word about it. She promised him but if that bitch came up against her she would have her buried underneath the jail.

"In case you haven't noticed, sweetie, I'm grown and this is my baby. That girl tried to cause me to lose my baby. What if it ends up having some type of birth defect? I'm dealing with this shit. I *will* be talking to the police. She deserves to be punished for what she's done. Hmph, this shit could have been prevented. Everybody put you on a pedestal like you're hot shit and invincible and no one get's past you. I can't tell. Nyse has been playing the both of you.

"I knew who she was immediately even with the *extra weight* and *red* hair. If anything that makes her stand out even more. Delaware is only but so big!" Bunny was becoming angrier and more courageous by the minute. She knew Fae couldn't do anything to her in the hospital.

The alarm on the monitors began to beep. The nurse hurried in. "Ma'am, is everything ok?" She came in and checked her vitals and the monitor. "Your blood pressure is rising and I need you to calm down. Can you two please keep her calm? We don't want to do anything that will cause harm to the child. She has already been through enough." She turned her attention back to Bunny. "There's an officer from the Wilmington Police department who would like to talk with you when you're ready." She said before exiting.

No this whore didn't! So you wanna break bad huh? Fae couldn't wait until the nurse exited the room. She was going to let that bitch have it. She stood up and made her way to her bedside. She gritted her teeth but was still able to speak calmly.

"I'm not one to repeat myself. So I'm gonna tell you this once, and only once. Don't you ever in your trashy life, talk to me the way you just did. I'm not one of these bitches in the streets. I could take your life at the snap of a finger because I don't give a fuck about you or that baby you're *supposed* to be carrying. You may have Brock fooled but I *been* caught on to your whore ass. You ain't shit! The only reason why you were with Kevin was for money. Now since he ain't got it like that you've been frontin' on him, acting all shitty. I've been watching your every move, that baby prolly ain't even his. Stinkin' Bitch, you think Nyse did something with that bottle? Fuck with me and your ass will be laying in Gracelawn."

Kevin went over towards Fae and grabbed her arm." Fae I want you to leave." He demanded.

She snatched away from him. "Are you fucking serious? You picking this Ho over me? We family…I've been there for your faggot ass since middle school! Taking up for your ass when you were getting chased home! Fucking up those bitches who talked shit about your little ass dick! You ain't shit without me nigga! I taught you everything you know. I fuckin' own your ass!

Kevin had heard enough. He was tired of Fae always trying to control his every move. He loved Bunny. She treated him better than

152

any woman had ever treated him. They were gonna be a family and if that met losing Fae, he was ready to do it. He believed everything happened for a reason, he lost Lil Kevin and gained a new child and he wasn't letting anyone stand in the way of his newfound happiness.

She stood in front of the door. *He can't be serious. He needs me. We're family. He just can't be serious.* Fae felt tears began to well up in her eyes. She waited a few more minutes to see if he was going to come out and apologize. He never came. She heaved a sigh. *That bitch is good as dead.* She thought as she walked away.

CHAPTER 25

The Payback

The ringing of the phone continued to blare in her ear. Nyse grumbled and put the pillow over top of her head. The phone had been ringing all morning long. She tried her best to ignore it but it just would not stop. *Damn who the fuck is calling me* this *early?* She picked the phone up and looked on the display. It read 15 missed calls. She checked the number and it was nobody but Corey. *What does he want?* She looked at the time and it was 3pm. She quickly sat up, and her head began to throb. *Aww shit.* She said grabbing her head. She had a hang over.

She held her head and rocked back and forth until the pain eased. She climbed out the bed and when her feet hit the floor she felt a little dizzy. She held onto the post trying to keep her balance. Her stomached burned. She held onto the wall for support as she made her way to the kitchen to get a bottle of water. She slumped over the counter and sipped her water.

Her body ached and she tried to remember what happened the night before. Then it all came back to her and a smile crept on her face. *I fucked that bitch up.* She laughed as she pictured Bunny on the floor balled up why she stomped her ass. Her goal was to stomp the baby out of her stomach. *Bitch gonna throw up in my face that she's knocked up by Kevin's little dick broke ass.* She really didn't appreciate her talking shit about her son. She picked up the house phone and called the baby sitter. She asked her to keep Kevin another night and she would pay her double. She promised herself that she would stop by and go check on Mop. She hadn't seen her since Mia's death. She felt her stomach grumble. She had to shit.

● ●

Bunny was held overnight for observation. Kevin sat at her side although he was there in body he was lost in his thoughts. Plots of vengeance flooded his mind. Nyse would utterly experience a crucial repercussion for what she had done to Bunny. To think he almost made her his wife made him feel ill. He knew she wasn't shit from the beginning. Now he wished he just stuck with the plan instead of trying to change her.

He thought if he showed her love the shell she had for a heart would be filled. Then there was Fae. He knew she wasn't going to give up on him that easily. He was all that she had left and he felt the same after his mom died. He had other family but she kept him sheltered from them. He felt that he owed her because she was the one who helped him rise to the status he had. He never thought of starting his own family until Nyse and the baby came along. At first it was just part of the plot but he started to enjoy being a family man. Having Li'l Kevin changed his outlook on life and his priorities began to shift too. The door opened and a tall white man who reminded him of "Lerch" from the Addams family walked in.

"Ms. Evans, everything is fine for now. However, keep in mind that you are still in your first trimester and that's a very fragile time. My recommendation to you is to first stay out of the clubs. Also, stay on bed rest for the next few weeks. You have an appointment on March 4th. You'll be entering into your second trimester by then if everything goes well." The doctor scribbled his instructions down and handed them to the nurse. "After you sign you're free to go."

A huge grin spread across Kevin's face. He reached for Bunny's hand but she snatched it away. She didn't seem happy about the news at all. He was confused. "Babe, what's wrong. Everything is fine. The baby's is going to be ok." He assured her.

Bunny climbed out of the bed and walked over to the chair to get her clothes from the brown bag. She dressed in silence while Kevin stared at her. She bent over to put on her boots but Kevin grabbed them up before she could reach them. She sucked her teeth. "What are you doing?"

"Sit down on the bed. You shouldn't be bending over." His words were gentle and caring. Bunny turned her head away and did as he asked.

She knew that he was a good guy but she didn't need the extra drama in her life. Especially since he was now broke, with money she could deal with the extra shit like Fae and Nyse. But she'd be damned if she was gonna sit around and be miserable for free. She was too old for that shit. She wished that she did lose the baby. That way, that bitch Nyse would catch a murder charge instead of a punk ass assault charge. She would also be rid of Kevin's ass. There would be no need for him to hang around without the baby being a factor. Her face grimaced at the thought of being pregnant and broke. *There's no way I'm doing this shit again, this baby gotta go even if I have to take matters into my own hands.*

• •

"Babe, I gotta go handle some business. I shouldn't be more than two hours. Make sure you stay off your feet. I'll bring dinner home." He kissed her on the lips and helped her out the car. He was about to help her up the steps but she wouldn't allow it.

"Brock, I'm not handicapped! You act like I ain't never been pregnant before!" She snapped. He watched her until she was in the house safely.

He went back into his car and pulled off. He didn't take the change in her attitude personally. He knew she was still upset. He believed she had every right to be. He was pissed too. Nyse went too far this time. He couldn't wait to get his hands around her neck. His

156

thoughts went to his son. He couldn't believe he was right under his nose and he didn't know it. She hadn't been to the house because everything was still in the same place. The season had changed so none of the baby's clothes wouldn't have been any good to him anyway. He wondered how big the baby was and if he was crawling yet or got his first tooth. He couldn't wait to get him back, so he could raise both of his kids together.

He turned onto Concord Avenue and drove slowly past the house where he last saw her. A gnawing feeling came over him. For some reason he could sense her presence. He checked out the scenery and his heart began to beat wildly when he saw this chick with long black hair, walking in the opposite direction. When she got closer he realized it wasn't her. Then he remembered that Bunny described her as being thick with red hair. He couldn't picture Nyse being thick and definitely couldn't imagine her with red hair. He knew she had to be going through something because the Nyse he knew was in love with her image. *Maybe that bitch is getting high.* He thought. He shook that idea.

Not Nyse, she was a lot of things and did a lot of dumb things but getting high was not one of them. He sat at the light in a trance. The honking of irate drivers interrupted his thoughts. He rolled down the window and cursed at the driver behind him. He didn't even notice who was driving the gold Honda Accord that whizzed past him.

• •

I just need to close my eyes and jump and then it will be all over. Bunny stood at the top of the steps, trying to psych herself up. She knew it was an act of desperation but she had to do it. She couldn't allow herself to stay pregnant another day. She closed her eyes and bent her knees to leap forward. As soon as she was about to go for it she heard the door open. In fear that it may be her daughter she grabbed the rail for support. *Damn, just when I got up enough nerve.* She continued down the stairs to greet her child.

"Tae?" She called her name. She reached the bottom and peaked in the living room and didn't see anyone.

I know I heard that door open. I ain't that damn crazy. She walked through the living room into the kitchen and no one was there. Confused, she walked back into the living room. She heard a door slam upstairs.

"Tae!" She yelled. *I don't have time for this, she play too damn much.* She figured her daughter was playing one of her many games trying to scare her. Bunny wasn't in the mood to be playing. She marched up the steps. "Tae, I'm not feeling this today! Answer me!"

There was no reply. She walked towards her bedroom and noticed the door was slightly ajar. A strange feeling overcame her. She noticed reddish brown puddles that resembled blood on the floor. She walked through the door slowly.

"Tae?' She said quietly. Once she was through the door her heart broke into a million pieces. "Oh my God, my, baby!" There laid her child on her blood soaked bed. She ran over to her and the door slammed. She turned around and looked her child's killer in the eyes. "I hate you!! I fucking hate you! She didn't do anything to you! She didn't do…. anything!" She cried as she hugged her dead child.

She watched Bunny as she mourned her child. She didn't feel a bit of pity. She walked towards her with her right hand behind her back. "I call it a tit for a tat. You took someone I loved from me, so it was only right that I return the favor." She smiled wickedly. She patted her on the head. "Don't cry sweetie, y'all will be together again sooner that you think."

She then pulled the bloody hammer from behind her back and swung it striking her in the throat. Bunny gasp as the blood sprayed out. The claw of the hammer was stuck. Fae pulled until it ripped through tearing muscles and tissue leaving behind a gaping hole exposing her insides. Blood flowed like a waterfall. Fae felt all warm inside as she watched Bunny's eyes role behind her head. "I told you not to fuck with me!" She pulled the red wig from her head, pulled the scissors from her back pocket and cut a strand and placed it in Bunny's hand.

CHAPTER 26

Mop

Nyse sat on the porch talking with Mop. To her surprise Mop was looking pretty good. Her hair was freshly relaxed and styled neatly. She had on new clothes and her face had a radiant glow giving her a youthful look. Now she could tell where Mia got her looks.

"I'm so happy for you Mop-Mop. What you did took a lot of courage. Most people would have gotten deeper in their habit. You know depression is a killer but you turned your negative into a positive and that's wonderful. I'm proud of you." She gave her a big hug and kissed her on her cheek.

Mop smiled sweetly. "Thank you. It wasn't easy. I wanted to die when my Mia was taken away. But at her funeral, that preacher spoke about how God gives and takes away. I know it sounds crazy but I believe that his way of getting my attention was taking my only child. I know I wasn't the best mom and that she did a lot of things she shouldn't have to get us what we needed. I didn't appreciate her when she was here and when you don't appreciate the gifts that God gives you he'll take them away. Mia was my gift. I didn't appreciate her and now that she's gone I can't get her back." A few tears escaped from her eyes.

Nyse felt a lump forming in her throat. She didn't believe it was God who took her away. It was her fault.

"Mop, I wish I could have changed that night. Everything happened so fast but if I wasn't being selfish, Mia would still be here." She cried.

Mop shook her head. "No, nothing you could have done would have changed the outcome. It was her time to go and I'm fine with it. I miss her. I miss her so much. But if she didn't die, I may have never realized my faults and got myself together. I wouldn't be sitting here talking to you with a clear mind and conscious." She sat still for a moment in deep thought. "How's everything between you and B.I?" She asked changing the subject.

Nyse wiped her eyes. "We...were fine. I saw more of him when we were downstate but since we've been back here he's back to the normal disappearing acts. Why you ask?"

"Do you two ever talk...about your past, y'alls family, or the future?" Mop asked.

"Well, at first we didn't. He was real secretive for a minute...I mean I wasn't all that honest with him either. I lied to him about my child's father. I eventually told him the truth. That the father was that dude Rashawn Gibbs. We shared a lot of personal things. B.I told me that him and his mother wasn't close but she passed and he doesn't know what happened to his little brother. As for our future, I don't know. He's not home enough for us to discuss it much." She said feeling uneasy about spilling personal details of her life.

"Nyse, I think you should really play close attention to him and really get to know him. I love B.I, like my own son. His mother and I were really close at one point but after I took him in we fell apart. She just didn't understand him, nobody does. I don't even understand him but I love him. I've grown to care about you too but you pay close attention to the details when people speak, there's always truths hidden."

Mop was talking in riddles. The last person who began to talk all crazy to her like that was her best friend Kee and that was right before the shit hit the fan. She listened carefully and took heed to her words.

"I'm 'bout to go in here and fry this chicken. You stayin' to eat right?" Nyse cheesed. "Yeah I'm staying I miss your chicken." She laughed.

All of a sudden sirens began to sound off from every direction. They both turned their heads as 3 cop cars flew down the avenue turning onto Washington. An ambulance and more cop cars went down Washington Street. They both looked at each other in confusion.

"I ain't hear no gunshots, did you?" Mop shook her head no and they went in the house.

• •

What done happened now? Kevin tried to turn onto Bunny's street but it was blocked off by what seemed to be 20 police cars and two ambulances. People were all in the streets watching. There was a traffic jam in both directions. Kevin dipped down the alley way and temporarily parked his car. He grabbed the bags from Red Lobster and started up the street. When he reached the crowd he noticed a lot of people staring at him and whispering. He didn't pay it any mind he just kept towards the house.

"Yo, Brock come mere' Dawg, I need to holla at you real quick!" A voice yelled through the crowd. He noticed it was his boy Roc. He walked over towards him and they met half way. They gave each other a pound and hugged. Kevin went to pull away but Roc held on to him.

"Walk with me. We need to talk." He said. Kevin broke loose.

"Yo nigga, what's wrong with you?" He laughed. "You aight?" He noticed the solemn look on his face.

Roc exhaled deeply while he chose how to deliver the devastating news to his best friend. "Yo, man, I don't even know how to say this." He put his hand on his shoulder for comfort. "Bunny and Tae are gone, man." He blurted.

Kevin backed away from him. "Gone? What the fuck you mean by gone? I just dropped her off less than an hour ago. Where could she have went?" His mind wouldn't allow him to register what Roc was trying to tell him. All of the chaos around him was in place for him to easily catch onto what he meant by *gone* but he was in denial.

Roc reached for him. "Man, they gone.... like gone and ain't no coming back." Kevin's attention went towards the house.

He tried to grasp what he was seeing but it didn't make sense to him. The yard was marked with crime scene tape and overtaken by a swarm of officers. What finally made him snap back to reality was the coroner carrying out a black body bag. At that moment he dropped the bags of food he was carrying and broke through the crowd heading towards the house. Roc was right on his tracks because he knew how his boy was when he was upset and he didn't want him catching a murder charge or worse. Ending up dead for wilding out on the police.

Kevin pushed past an officer and attempted to run up the steps to the house.

"Hey you can't go up there this is a restricted area!" The cop shouted.

"Fuck you nigga this is my house! My pregnant wife is in there!" He barked.

A few of the other officers heard what was going on and went in after him with weapons drawn. Roc stopped in his tracks. He was on the run and he didn't want any run-ins with the law. He backed away and disappeared back into the crowd.

Kevin didn't make it past the front door. He was surrounded. His mind told him to surrender but his heart said otherwise. "I just need to see my wife! She's pregnant. I just brought her home from the hospital this morning." He pleaded.

A tall black man broke through the circle and flashed him his badge. "My name is Detective Daniels and I would like to ask you some questions concerning your *wife*." He looked Kevin over and knew damn well he wasn't the victim's husband. "Come with me."

"I ain't goin' no fucking where! I need to see my wife!" He demanded.

"Ok, not a problem follow me."

He went inside the house and Kevin followed behind him. They went up the stairs into Tae's room. He opened the door and allowed Kevin to enter first. He studied Kevin's reaction.

He walked over to get a closer look at the damage that was done. Her throat was ripped out completely. *Unfucking believable this is not happening.* He knew no one else could have done this except Fae. He choked back tears, not just for Bunny but also for his unborn child. There was no way he could let Fae get away with this. He wasn't into snitching but he knew there was no way he could go up against her alone. She would be waiting for him and he knew he was no match for her.

He turned to the detective. "You got any leads on who may have done this?" He asked.

Detective Daniels pulled a plastic bag from his jacket pocket. "I was just about to ask you the same thing. Does this ring a bell? Do you know who this hair may belong to? It was in the victim's grip. She must of grabbed it trying to defend herself. " He handed Kevin an evidence bag that contained a few strands of red hair. Kevin thought for a moment. *Red hair...why is that familiar to me?* Then it came to him.

"No way!" He looked back at Bunny's mangled body and looked back at the bag. *Nyse ain't built like that, she couldn't have done this.*

"Is there something you need to tell me, son?"

Kevin shook his head. "Naw. This don't mean nothing to me!" He handed the bag back to the detective and hurriedly walked away. He realized exiting in a hurry made him look like a suspect, but time was of the essence. He had to find Nyse.

"Hold up son, I'm not done talking to you." He followed Kevin trying to catch up with him. "I'm warning you son if you know anything and you're not telling us I'll charge you with conspiracy and obstruction of justice!"

Kevin detoured into Bunny's room and headed towards the window. He wasn't telling them shit. He knew they weren't going do anything. They would chalk it up as another unsolved case. The same way they did Rashawn and all the others. He wasn't letting Nyse get away with murdering his child. He opened the window.

"Don't move! Or I swear I'll shoot your black ass!" The detective yelled. Kevin froze for a moment. He already had one foot on the fire escape step. He glared at the detective. "Fuck you!" He said before jumping completely out the window.

"Fuck!" He ran over to the window and watched Kevin jump over the back fence.

•••

"Cousin, let me talk to you for a minute."

Nyse took a hit of her blunt and blew the smoke in the air. He came over to her with a big grin on his face. Today his hair was braided in two cornrows on the side of his head.

"What's up, Nyse?"

"You tell me? What's this I'm hearing about you getting married? Nigga we the same age how you gonna go and get married? Who is she anyway?" She said with much attitude.

Cousin laughed. "Man, shut the fuck up! You just mad cause B.I ain't ask your ass to marry him!" He joked.

Nyse turned her nose up. "Please! Who said I wanted to be married to B.I? He got too much shit going on. Plus I'm too young I need to see the world. Besides I'm gonna be a high profile lawyer like Johnny Cochran and I can't be married to no street thugs. I'mma get me a nigga in a Brooks Brother suit with an Ivy League education. He gonna wear wire rimmed glasses and everything." She said in confidence.

He started bagging up.

"What, nigga?"

"I'm serious!" She said trying to convince him.

"So you gonna marry a lame ass nigga huh? How the fuck you think you gonna pull that off when you can't even stop smoking? You ain't even been to college, how you gonna be a lawyer chick?"

"Aight, you watch! You gonna be sitting in jail and you gonna need my ass to get you off and I'm gonna laugh at you just like you laughin' at me right now!" Nyse inhaled and blew the smoke in his face. "You just watch!"

"Go ahead with that bullshit. Look I'm about to be out. Me and my baby are ready to head to the movies. I'll see you later, Johnny." He joked.

Nyse finished smoking her blunt and emerged from the side of the house. She began to get in her feelings. *I can't believe he don't think I got what it takes to be a lawyer. I guess that nigga don't know I was a straight "A" student all through high school. I had colleges begging to take me.* As she walked down the street she thought about all the events that had taken place in her life the last few years. Feelings of regret filled her. *I fucked up. I really fucked up.* She realized that her whole life could have been different if she would have just thought things through thoroughly instead of acting on impulse. She should have accepted responsibility for her own actions.

Her phone rang and it was Corey. She did feel bad for ducking him all day but she wasn't in the mood to speak to anyone. She hit the ignore button and the phone fell from her hand. She bent down to pick it up but it was kicked to the side. *What the fuck?* She felt herself being pulled up.

"Get the fuck off me." She snapped. She tried to free herself but she was high and her movements were sluggish.

She turned around to see who her attacker was. Kevin stood before her at least that's who she believed it to be. She had never seen him look the way he did. He smelled like he bathed in Seagram's. His eyes were red and his face was one of a mad man.

He pulled his chrome .357 magnum and said "Get the fuck in the car now, if you make any noise or try to run, your done!" He hissed.

Nyse looked around for help but of all nights the Ave was empty. She wanted to make a run for Mop's but she didn't want to get her caught up in anything. She knew Kevin was capable of killing.

She witnessed it first hand when he laid down Chauncey. She quietly entered the car against her will. He got in and pulled off.

"Kevin, look I'm sorry for what happened with Bunny. She was talking shit to me and I was drunk. I ain't one for no bitches talking crazy to me you know that. I guess I was a little jealous because she was talking shit about her having your baby and how you ain't want Lil Kevin no more." He took the butt of is gun and busted her in the jaw with the butt of the gun.

"Awww....Oh God!" She cried holding her face. Blood began to spill from her mouth.

"Stop lying, bitch!" He spat.

He pulled into the entrance of Brandywine Park and made his way towards the most secluded area. Once he was at his destination, he got out the car and pulled her out. Nyse was still holding her jaw. The pain from the blow shot straight to her head, which was throbbing out of control.

"Where's my fucking son? That's all I wanna know. Tell me where he is then I'll let you go." He said with the gun aimed at her temple.

"I...I can take you...to him." She slurred.

Her jaw was so loose the blood mixed with her saliva ran out her mouth making her sound as if she was suffering from some type of retardation. She was praying that he would take her to the house and B.I would be there so he can kill his ass. She couldn't believe that he was doing this to her over some bitch and baby that was most likely not even his.

Kevin didn't believe a word she said. He figured it was some type of set up. He became more furious that she tried to play high and mighty. He punched her in the face repeatedly, she fell to the ground and he kicked her in the head several more times.

"Bitch, you think I'm stupid? You tryna set me the fuck up and kill me like you killed my girl and baby? You know what...fuck that lil bastard! He's good as dead just like his dad you trifling, bitch. Fae was right about you! Just to think...I was gonna try and make you my

166

wife. Move you away and give you a better life. I should have killed your ass when you fucked the plans up with Nelson!" He backed away and cocked his gun but it was jammed.

Nyse was a bloody mess and her vision was blurred. She tried to drag her body away from him. She knew if she didn't get away he was going to kill her. She dug her nails into the dirt for leverage as she scooted across the ground. She didn't get far before she felt a blow to her mid back. She growled in pain.

"Where the fuck you think you goin', bitch?"

Kevin cocked the gun back again and it worked. "This is for my family!" A thunderous clap was the last thing Nyse heard before everything went black.

CHAPTER 27

The Reunion

Where did I go wrong? She watched the machine breathe life into a child they said was hers. Her face and body was swollen like a balloon. Her tongue hung out of her mouth allowing the tube to go down her throat. Her eyes told her it wasn't her. There was no way this red haired cocaine addict was her daughter. Deep inside she knew her little Nalyse was trapped somewhere in the stranger that laid before her.

She received the news two weeks ago from a Lt. Hamilton. He was the same officer who locked up her son. He informed her that her daughter was found beaten half to death with her boyfriends head splattered all over her body. Although she was angry with Nyse she never hated her. She just didn't know how to deal with the feelings she was having. She didn't really believe that she had Kat killed but she needed to blame somebody and Nyse was it.

She was already upset with her for what she did with Rashawn amongst other things so she was the easy target. A day didn't go by that she didn't think about her child or grandson. She just couldn't deal with her because it brought back too many memories that she wanted to bury. She dropped to the floor when they read her the report.

"Ma'am we found traces of cocaine and marijuana in her system and she's also carrying a child." The doctor told her. Lt. Hamilton held her up and tried to comfort her. If she didn't know any better he seemed to be disturbed by the news also.

She had ill feelings towards him at first. If it weren't for him her son wouldn't be facing life but deep inside she knew it was for the best. She rather him be in jail than to be dead. At least she could visit him. Lt. Hamilton sat with her and at her bedside until she got herself together. When he was about to go and she asked him to have someone bring her the baby. He assured her he would look into it immediately. Later that evening they brought Lil Kevin to the hospital and she was able to take him.

She was awarded temporary guardianship over him until his mother recovered. If she didn't recover, she would have him permanently. She didn't want to think that way she knew Nalyse was strong and she would pull through it. She had to pull through. She needed to make things right with her daughter. She didn't want her to die thinking she hated her. She walked over to the bed and rubbed her arm.

"Lyse baby, wake up…I miss you honey. Your son misses his mommy. I need you to get up. The baby's birthday is just a few weeks away and you need to be here to help him celebrate." She tried to sound cheerful but she was dying inside.

No response. The swelling seemed to go down a bit in her face but she still didn't look like her child. Her lips were huge and cracked to the point of bleeding. She was pissed.

"These hospitals are getting all this money and they can't even keep my baby's lips from being chapped." She retrieved some lipbalm from her pocketbook. When she looked up she noticed she wasn't alone.

"Good Morning Ms. Nyse." It was Lt. Hamilton."

"Morning? As you can see nothing has changed." She said flatly.

He knew he wasn't her favorite person but he was only doing his job at the time. He had been checking on Nyse around the clock. He wanted to get to her before anyone else did. She had a warrant for her arrest for the attack of Bonita Evans aka Bunny. Since Bunny turned up dead not even 24 hours after their altercation in the club.

She was now a suspect to her murder. He wanted to be the only one to deal with her especially since she could be carrying his child.

"Don't worry she's a fighter. She'll pull through it." He was optimistic. *She has to.* He thought. *For the sake of our baby.*

Ketura bent over the bed and applied the lip balm to Nyse's lips. "Its grape flavored mama. It's your favorite. Don't you want to taste it?" She teased

She felt something move underneath her body. She jumped back. Nyse's fingers were moving.

"Ahh…you see that?!" She moved!" She said excitedly. Corey ran over to see for himself. Her mother was right, she was moving. "Go get the doctor!" She ordered. Corey did as he was told.

"Come on baby! I know you hear me! Wake up Lyse!" She cried.

Nyse moved her head towards the direction of her voice and her eyes opened. She recognized the woman who stood before her. *Mom?* She tried to speak but there was something blocking the way. She lifted her hand towards her mouth and felt the tube and she tugged at it.

"No, no, no don't do that, baby! You need that to breathe." Her mother warned.

Breathe? What? Where am I what's going on? Nyse became belligerent and pulled the tube from her throat she gagged uncontrollably. She began to convulse and her mother tried to hold her down. The nursing staff and doctors rushed in at the nick of time to work on her.

• •

"Ms. Nyse, can we have a word with you?"

The doctor led the mother back into the room. Nyse was lying down peacefully. But she was no longer on the life support machine. She had IV's and oxygen flowing through her nose. She was relieved her baby was coming back to her.

"Is she ok?"

"Ma'am I am 100% sure she will make a full recovery. We did an ultra sound and the baby is doing well also. You can let her know she's having a little girl. She seems to be as tough as her mother." He smiled. "She's slightly sedated, so she may say things that don't make a lot of sense. She has a few fractures and we have her on fluid medicine to bring the swelling down. If she keeps up this way she may be home as early as next week." He assured her. That was music to her ears. She couldn't wait to bring her home so they could start over.

• •

Just as the doctors predicted Nyse was well enough to go home the following week. Nyse found it hard to believe that Kevin was gone. She could have sworn she was the one shot. She figured it had to be B.I who killed him but why would he just leave her there? *Maybe he thought I was already dead.*

She asked her mother who had been up to visit her at the hospital. B.I didn't even care enough to visit. She told her only Corey had been there. What really messed her up was that she had to take drug classes since they found cocaine in her system. She tried to tell them that she had never done cocaine she only smoked marijuana. That's when she was told that she could have been getting laced weed, or woolies. She remembered Mia saying that word before. She was pissed that no one told her exactly what a woolie was and even more pissed at B.I for giving it to her. Especially since she was carrying a baby. She didn't want a cocaine-addicted child, Lil Kevin had enough issues. A second baby with problems would've been too much.

That was another blow she faced, a baby. She didn't plan on having any more kids any time soon.

"I'm ready mom." She sat in the wheel chair and signed her last discharge paper.

"Ok, baby. Let me grab this bag." Her mother said.

Just as they were ready to depart they were interrupted.

"Nalyse Nyse, you have the right to remain silent…"

An officer pulled her up from the wheel chair and handcuffed her.

"What the fuck is this shit?" She snapped.

"You can't do this! She's still not well! She was turning herself in next week!" Her mother pleaded.

Nyse looked at her mom like she was crazy. *What is she talking about? Turning myself in for what?* The information that she was about to be hit with was enough to have made her want to stay in the coma a little while longer.

CHAPTER 28

Sleeping With The Enemy

Detective Daniels sat with his legs crossed waiting patiently for Nyse to talk. He had her in custody for 3 hours and she didn't say a word. "Now Ms. Nyse, you making things worse for yourself by not talking. There are 3 people that are now dead and they all had something in common...you. Now I can make things easier for you if you can tell me what happened."

Nyse ignored him. She sipped her water and rolled her eyes. She didn't have shit to say to him, especially without a lawyer. She didn't know what was taking her mother so long. She gave her the key to the safe deposit box so she could get her money and an attorney.

Daniels stood up. He knew he was getting nowhere with her. He had a trick to get her to talk. He went out the door and returned moments later with a manila folder. He opened it up and sat it in the middle of the table. Nyse glanced at it and then did a double take. She pulled the folder closer to her and read the name under the mug shot. *Eric R. Gibbs. Gibbs?* She jumped up from the table and threw the folder.

"This is bullshit! There's no way! There's no way!"

"There's no way what? There's no way that you've been sleeping with your son's uncle? Hmmm...Is that it?" He said being sarcastic.

Nyse thought hard about everything that she and B.I talked about. The more she thought about it the more it fit together. *That's why he was so into Lil' Kevin. Then she thought about Ms. Gibbs. That was his sick relative he was visiting.*

"No, no, nooo!" She screamed. She balled up on the floor and cried.

She couldn't believe she was carrying yet another Gibbs child. He played her all that time. *Why didn't he just kill me? He knew who I was from the beginning. He turned me out on coke and made me believe he loved me.*

"Ms. Nyse, get up sweetheart. It's ok. We can help you if you help us. Mr. Gibbs is a very dangerous man. We have been looking for him for years. When we searched your address, we found some of his belongings and fingerprints. Again, he's extremely dangerous and we would like you to help us put him behind bars for good. We believe he may be responsible for murdering Mr. Brockman. We just need your cooperation. He helped her up to her feet and she went over to her seat.

He picked up the folder and turned to the back a pulled out a few more pictures of a hanging burned corpse. "Do you know who that is?" He asked.

She couldn't speak and she shook her head no.

He pulled out another picture. "I know you know who this is." It was Caree. "I know her."

"Well this is what she looks like now. We believe Eric is responsible for committing this murder. Caree, as well as yourself didn't get along with his mother all that great. He must have found out she was responsible for her death. However, that didn't sit too well with us. What could she have done to Caree to cause her to have her brutally attacked? But, Ms. Gibbs *did do* something to you. Didn't she? She was trying to take her grandchild from you."

"I'll talk...but not to you. I want to speak with Lt. Corey Hamilton."

● ●

Two hours later Corey was at Nyse's side. She told him she was ready to talk about what she knew about her sister's murder. But she had some demands of her own before she spoke. She retold him her story. Her entire story. Everyone sat in awe. They couldn't believe all the information one person was withholding. She told on everybody from the twins being responsible for Ms. Gibbs death to Fae being responsible for the murder of her sister. She even told on Hause and Cousin. She was pissed because they didn't even visit her in the hospital not one time. Jab even sent flowers they didn't do anything.

"Thank you for your cooperation. I have one question for you. Why would you hold all of this information inside? Do you know how many lives could have been spared if you just told someone about this months ago?" Daniels was disgusted.

Corey turned his head away. He was feeling guilty because he knew everything too.

"I don't know. I just want all of this to be over. I gotta warn you about Fae. She doesn't look like she could hurt a fly but that bitch is deadly and slick. You need to hurry up if you're going to catch her. She has all types of connections on the inside. How come you think she's never been caught?" She said fearfully.

She wanted her behind bars immediately especially after she heard what she did to Bunny. A nurse from the hospital told them about the confrontation that went on in Bunny's hospital room the night before she killed her. The fibers from the red hair that they found turned out to be synthetic. That's what saved Nyse since all of her hair was real.

"We'll get on it. We'll have to keep you in protective custody until your transfer is ready. No one in this department besides Lt. Hamilton and myself will know where you're located. You're getting a fresh start, even though you don't deserve it. Just don't fuck this up!" He stormed out.

"I'm not taking my son. I want him to stay with my mother. She's grown attached to him. She's losing me again, so I want her to have something to remember me by."

Corey laughed. "You act like your gonna be gone forever. You can come back once it's safe."

"Yeah I guess so." She didn't have much confidence in their system. B.I had been on the run for years and they still haven't caught up to him.

"I have a question. I know this is not the best time to be asking this but what are you going do about *our* baby? I know you'll be away and I would like to be there when she's born."

Nyse held her head down. She wasn't ready to discuss the baby thing. She wasn't even sure if it was his. "I'm gonna have to be honest with you. I'm not sure if you're the father of this child or not. If you want this baby for you and your wife your more than welcome to take her though. I'm not ready to be a fulltime mom. I'm not sure if I ever will be."

Corey walked away from the table. He wasn't prepared to hear that the child may not be his. He didn't know about taking the child home to his wife either. *What if the baby is mine and she looks just like me? How will I be able to explain this to my wife?* He decided he would work something out when and if the time comes. The door opened up and a female officer came in.

"Ms. Nyse, we are ready to transport you now."

"Wait! She didn't even have a chance to say goodbye to her mother or son." Corey stood in front of Nyse like he was shielding her. Nyse stood up.

"It's ok. I'm ready. Just do me a favor and tell my mother that I love her and give my son a kiss for me. I think it's better this way. If I see her it will just make things harder and I don't want her to know anything that may cause her or my son to be in any danger." She gave Corey a hug. "Thank you for everything and I'll see you soon." She gave him a kiss on the cheek. She turned to the officer who greeted her with a smile. "I'm ready to go."

When they left out the door a feeling of relief came over her. She thought about what Mop said to her about God taking things away from you to get your attention. She almost lost her life and that

176

was a wake up call and a half. She was living recklessly and didn't appreciate life. Now she had a second chance and she was going to do things the right way.

MAY 2002

I can't believe this day is finally here, my graduation day. Nyse went over to her closet and pulled out her Black Jones of New York Suit she was wearing underneath her robe. She was filled with joy. She checked the time, she had a hour to shower and dress before her fiancé Byron would be there to pick her up. They had been dating for the last 2 years. At first she was hesitant to date anyone. She was still trying to find herself and didn't want to fall into any of her old habits.

The first year was hard for her to transition from being free to being confined to one area. Since she was pregnant she couldn't start full right away so they sent her out to the Midwest in the witness protection program. She thought she was about to go crazy. She wasn't sure if she made the right decision. She couldn't call anyone but it wasn't like there was anyone left for her to call. After the baby was born, they transported her to her new residence, Georgetown University. Things went smoothly from then on.

After the third year all thoughts of going back to Delaware faded. They never caught B.I or Fatal, so she was stuck. Sometimes she was afraid they would find her. Corey assured her that would never happen. Everyone thought she passed away. Corey told her mother the truth he just didn't tell her where she was located. She wanted so bad to reach out to her. She wondered how big Lil' Kevin was and how he looked.

Corey kept his word, he took her daughter who she name

Corah. It turned out that he wasn't the father. He had a DNA test done. So Eric was definitely the father. He sent her pictures on every holiday. Things were better between him and his wife so she didn't hear from him as often. He made sure his mother had a relationship with her granddaughter too. He hired her as his babysitter, so she could spend time with her. She just wished her mother and kids could be there to share this special day with her.

She went into the bathroom to turn on the water for her shower. The doorbell rang. *I wonder who that is?* She grabbed a robe she had hanging on the back of the bathroom door and put it on. The doorbell rang again. *"Coming"* she sang.

She wasn't expecting any company so she figured it was Byron. He must have forgotten his key. She looked through the peephole and she didn't see anyone. She cracked the door open and noticed a small package sitting in front of her door. She reached down and picked it up. She stepped out in her hallway and looked over the rail to see if anyone was there. It was empty. She walked back to her apartment and went inside. She looked at the box and it didn't have a card or anything attached. She shook it and it made a clanking noise. She smiled. *Jewelry! Thank you, Byron.* She figured he had it delivered. He always did little things like that. She tore the package open.

She took the lid off the box. Her smile faded when she pulled out the blood stained *Poison* necklace that she received from Littlez more than five years ago. She threw it across the room and cringed in fear. *How the hell did that get here?!* She hadn't seen that necklace since the night Kevin tried to kill her. She jumped up from the couch and ran to the kitchen. She picked up the phone to call Corey but the phone was dead. She heard a door slam from her bedroom area. She pulled open her knife drawer and grabbed the biggest one she could find. She backed out of the kitchen keeping her eyes glued on her bedroom door.

Everything is going to be ok. Somebody is just trying to fuck with me. She tried convincing herself. She backed into the coffee table causing her to lose her balance. She fell to the floor and the knife fell from her hand. She jumped to her feet swiftly and went for her knife but it wasn't there. She turned around and screamed. Eric put his hands around her mouth and put the knife to her throat.

"Damn, babe, is that how you treat your baby's daddy?" Nyse squeezed her eyes shut hoping that when she opened them it would all be a bad dream. She wouldn't be so lucky when she opened them Fae was standing before her. This was a nightmare.

"Hey chica! Long time no see!" She laughed.

Eric threw her to the couch. The two stood before her. "How did you find me? No one was supposed to know where I was."

"Are you serious? I knew where you were from the beginning. I knew when you were in Kansas. I was at the hospital when you had the baby. I even knew the day you arrived here. By the way, the new boyfriend is real cute. A little too lame for me though." Fae sat next to her and patted Nyse's leg. "He really likes you too. He just didn't understand why you never told him about your brother and sister. I told him we were surprising you by coming down for your graduation and we would bring you for him. So there was no need for him to pick you up."

Nyse began to cry. "Please tell me you didn't hurt him."

"No, honey we let him go. Besides, we wouldn't do anything like that with the kids in the car."

"Kids? Oh no! Don't hurt my babies!" She pleaded.

Eric found her statement amusing "Your babies? That's funny I didn't think you gave a fuck about them especially when you gave them away. Your mom…She cared though. She gave her life trying to protect them."

"You fucking bastard you killed my mom? She didn't do anything! Why?! Why?!" She cried.

"The same reason why you had mine killed!"

"She tried to take my child."

Nyse sat numb. Everything she did was coming back to her.

Someone walked through the front door. They all turned around and the two both drew their guns quickly. "Damn, it's just me!

180

Lil' Kevin had to pee." The female walked in holding both of the kid's hands. Nyse's heart broke into a million pieces. Both of her children where in arms reach. She looked at the female closely and realized she knew her from somewhere. "Nyse, where's the bathroom? Kevin gotta pee." She said smacking her gum.

"I know you. I know who you are! Nurse Lynn! You're the chick from Leroy's" Nyse said.

"You are so right, didn't I tell you his fuck game was serious." She winked her eye and took the kids to the back.

Nyse was confused. "She's the one who told me to talk to you…how do you…I don't understand!"

"Lynn is my wife." Both Fae and Nyse's face dropped.

"Married, when the fuck did you get married?" Fae snapped." You keeping secrets from me now, why didn't you tell me?"

"The same reason why you didn't tell me you were the one who killed my brother! You thought I would never find out? I knew everything from the beginning. My mom called and filled me in on everything. I knew who that bitch was the night I met her at Leroy's. I thought she was the one who had my brother killed. I knew it was you when that girl tried to talk and you set her on fire all quick. I knew you were hiding shit then. You lied and said you didn't know where my nephew was but that the whole time your bitch ass brother had him. That's why I killed his ass that night. I was gonna kill the bitch too but something told me to wait, thank God I did or I would never have my Lil mama."

Fae couldn't believe what she was hearing. All this time Eric was playing the both of them. Lynn came back in. "Baby, you need to hurry up we need to get on the road. Nyse, good seeing you again. I promise your kids will be well taken care of and maybe I'll tell them about you one day." She winked and was out the door.

Fae sat on the edge of the couch. She was dumbfounded. She was usually on top of her game. Nyse watched the both of them care- fully. She was fuming. There was no way that she was going to let them leave with her kids. She noticed Fae's gun dangling. *This bitch is slippin'*. Nyse sprang to her feet and quickly grabbed at the gun. Fae was already on it. Nyse didn't even see it coming. Fae shot her straight between the eyes the same way she had killed Kat. Nyse's body slumped to the floor.

"YO!! What the fuck is you doing? That wasn't the plan!" Eric snapped. His intentions were for her to die a slow painful death.

"No nigga you didn't follow the plan. I can't you believe you! You just played me. So I guess you were gonna just kill me too, when you were done huh?"

Eric grinned devilishly. "Uhh...Yeah, pretty much."

Fae couldn't believe it. Never in a million years did she think her mentor, the only person she really ever trusted, would be the one to end her life. She looked at the bag of "tricks" he had sitting next to him. *I can't go out like that.* She refused to let him get the satisfaction of seeing her suffer.

"I...I can't let you do that!" She closed her eyes and put the gun to her mouth and pulled the trigger.

Eric jumped up. "No!!! You stupid bitch!"

He went over and kicked Fae's dead body. He was furious. He wanted to be the one to kill her. He stood over both dead bodies and pulled his dick out and pissed on them. He had to get some satisfaction out of it. He picked the necklace up off the floor. He lifted Nyse's head and placed it around her neck. He looked over at Nyse one last time and snickered. He had to admit she was most definitely Poison.

The End

Cartel Publications Order Form
www.thecartelpublications.com
Inmates ONLY get novels for $10.00 per book!

Titles	Fee
Shyt List	_____ $15.00
Shyt List 2	_____ $15.00
Pitbulls In A Skirt	_____ $15.00
Pitbulls In A Skirt 2	_____ $15.00
Victoria's Secret	_____ $15.00
Poison	_____ $15.00
Poison 2	_____ $15.00
Hell Razor Honeys	_____ $15.00
Hell Razor Honeys 2	_____ $15.00
A Hustler's Son 2	_____ $15.00
Black And Ugly As Ever	_____ $15.00
Year of The Crack Mom	_____ $15.00
The Face That Launched A Thousand Bullets	_____ $15.00
The Unusual Suspects	_____ $15.00
Miss Wayne & The Queens of DC	_____ $15.00

Please allow 5-7 business days for delivery. The Cartel is not responsible for prison orders rejected.

(CARTEL CAFÉ AND BOOKS STORE REQUESTS)
Inmates we are now accepting order requests for ANY PAPERBACK BOOK you want outside of the Cartel Titles. Books will be shipped directly from our bookstore. If it's in print, we can get it! We are NOT responsible for books out of print. For Special Order Requests, Please send $15.00 and the name of book below. To prevent refund if 1st special request novel is out of print, please include 2nd requested novel in case the other is unavailable.
SORRY, NO STAMPS ACCEPTED WITH SPECIAL ORDERS!

Please add $4.00 per book for shipping and handling. NO PERSONAL CHECKS ACCEPTED!

The Cartel Publications * P.O. Box 486 * Owings Mills * MD * 21117

Name: _____

Address: _____

_____

Contact#/Email: _____

THE CARTEL COLLECTION

The Cartel Collection
Established in January 2008
We're growing stronger by the month!!!

www.thecartelpublications.com